The Best of
GIRLS
to the
RESCUE®

The Best of
GIRLS
to the
RESCUE®

Tales of clever, courageous girls
from around the world

Edited by Bruce Lansky

⚏ Meadowbrook Press

Distributed by Simon & Schuster
New York

Library of Congress Catalog Card Number: 97-645111

ISSN 1089-5442
Publisher's ISBN: 0-88166-427-8
Simon & Schuster Ordering # 0-689-02468-1

Editor: Bruce Lansky
Editorial Director: Christine Zuchora-Walske
Proofreader: Megan McGinnis
Production Manager: Paul Woods
Cover Illustrator: Joy Allen

pp. 1, 41, 107, 169, and 267 "The Fairy Godmother's Assistant," "Liza and the Lost Letter," "Grandma Rosa's Bowl," "Kim's Surprise Witness," and "The Royal Joust" © 1995 by Bruce Lansky; p. 15 "Troop 13 to the Rescue" © 2000 by Penny Warner; p. 33 "The Clever Daughter" © 1998 by Martha Johnson; p. 51 "Keesha and the Rat" © 1997 by Jack Kelly; p. 59 "Young Maid Marian and Her Amazing, Astounding Pig" © 1996 by Stephen Mooser; p. 73 "Dingo Trouble" © 1998 by Debra Tracy; pp. 85, 125, and 245 "Kamala and the Thieves," "Sarah's Pickle Jar," and "Maya's Stone Soup" © 1996 by Bruce Lansky; p. 95 "Fishing for Trouble" © 1997 by Sandy Cudmore; p. 111 "Railroad Through and Through" © 1998 by Cynthia Mercati; p. 131 "On the Way to Broken Bow" © 2000 by Marianne J. Dyson; p. 145 "Temper, Temper" © 1997 by Bruce Lansky; p. 161 "Tulia!" © 1998 by Joan Harries; p. 177 "For Love of Sunny" © 1984 by Vivian Vande Velde. Original version first appeared in *Once Upon a Test: Three Light Tales of Love* by Vivian Vande Velde (Albert Whitman & Co., 1984); p. 185 "Emily and the Underground Railroad" © 1996 by Joanne Mitchell; p. 199 "Carla and the Greedy Merchant" © 1995 by Robert Scotellaro; p. 205 "Vassilisa the Wise" © 1995 by Joanne Mitchell; p. 219 "Savannah's Piglets" © 1995 by Sheryl Nelms; p. 231 "Shannon Holmes's First Case" © 1999 by Stephen Mooser; p. 255 "The Peacemakers" © 1995 by Lois Greiman.

Published by Meadowbrook Press, 5451 Smetana Drive, Minnetonka, MN 55343
www.meadowbrookpress.com

BOOK TRADE DISTRIBUTION by Simon & Schuster, a division of Simon and Schuster, Inc., 1230 Avenue of the Americas, New York, NY 10020

06 05 04 03 02   12 11 10 9 8 7 6 5 4 3 2 1

Printed in the United States of America

Dedication

This book is dedicated to my daughter, Dana. I used to make up stories when she was young, hoping to inpsire her to believe in herself and pursue her dreams. It is in that spirit that I have written and collected the stories in this series.

Acknowledgments

Thank you to the over one hundred young women who served on reading panels for the Girls to the Rescue series.

Contents

Introduction

If you're curious about why I decided nearly eight years ago to start a series of books featuring clever, courageous girls, I can rattle off five good reasons: "Cinderella," "Snow White," "Sleeping Beauty," "Rapunzel," and "The Princess and the Pea."

These fairy tales were written one hundred and fifty to two hundred years ago—before most princes had joined the ranks of the unemployed, and before women had landed jobs as rocket scientists, brain surgeons, and VJs on MTV.

The stories that appear in Girls to the Rescue are very different from traditional fairy tales. The girls featured in the series' seven books are not only smart, they're also spunky enough to come through when the going gets tough. And the response to the series from girls, parents, teachers, booksellers, and reviewers has been overwhelmingly positive.

For *The Best of Girls to the Rescue*, I selected twenty-five stories that rise above the rest. If you like stories about danger and excitement, or if you love to read stories about heroes from all over the world who use their brains to triumph over adversity, then this is the book for you.

I hope that you enjoy these stories so much, you'll want to share them. I also hope that after reading them, you are motivated to think about how you, like the heroes in this book, can help your family, friends, and country.

Bruce Lansky

The Fairy Godmother's Assistant

AN ORIGINAL STORY BY BRUCE LANSKY

When you need help, don't you wish a fairy godmother would suddenly appear to make things right?
Well, don't hold your breath. She doesn't do that kind of
thing anymore. (She's getting on in years, you know.)
So if you want some help—she still fixes anything from
broken windows to broken hearts—you'll have to visit
her little cottage in the Bavarian woods and wait your
turn, just like everyone else. And when you knock on
the door, I'll let you in and make you comfortable. I'll
even serve you a nice cold glass of lemonade.

You see, I'm the fairy godmother's assistant.

My job used to be quite simple, really, until the fairy
godmother announced she would be taking a much-needed

vacation. I was scared stiff! What would I say to people who came for help? I didn't know any magic. I couldn't have turned a pumpkin into a glittering coach if my life depended on it.

"Don't worry," the fairy godmother told me. "You're very sensible. I'm sure you'll find a way to handle whatever comes up. And besides, I'll only be gone for a few days."

To be honest, I didn't get much sleep that night. I kept wondering how I could possibly fill her shoes.

I got up early the next morning and went to the kitchen to make a fresh pitcher of lemonade. When I heard a knock at the door, I opened it and found a young woman with a tear-stained face, wearing a tattered old dress. I explained that the fairy godmother would be gone for a few days and that I was her assistant. But she looked so sad that I invited her in for a glass of lemonade to cheer her up.

As soon as she sat down, she started to cry. I sat beside her and gave her a handkerchief to dry her eyes. "First wipe away your tears. Then tell me what's bothering you," I said in a soothing voice.

The young woman took a few deep breaths before speaking. "My name is Ella, but my stepmother and stepsisters call me Cinder-Ella, because my apron is always covered with cinders from cleaning the fireplace. They are mean to me and make me clean the house, cook, sew, and run errands all day while they have fun. Now I have to make them new gowns for the royal ball. But I want to go, too." She started to cry again.

I could guess where this was leading. "I'm very sorry to hear that," I responded. "I suppose you came to ask the fairy godmother to get you to the ball. Is that it?"

She nodded.

"I wish I could help you, but I make lemonade, not magic."

Ella began to cry again. "Can't you do anything?"

"There's not much I can do. It's really up to you."

She dried her eyes again with the handkerchief and stared at me in amazement. "Up to me?" she queried.

"It's really very simple," I said. "If you want to go to the ball, go. And don't let anything or anyone stop you."

"But how can I go to the ball without an evening gown?"

"Don't look at me," I responded. "You're the seamstress. If you can make gowns for your two stepsisters, why not make another for yourself?"

Ella pondered this for a while, then shook her head. "But I can't afford to buy silk or velvet. How can I make a gown without any fabric?"

"Are there any velvet curtains in your house? Or silk bed sheets?"

Her worried look slowly turned into a smile. "There sure are!" she gushed. But her smile was short-lived. Another question had flashed into her mind. "But what about dancing slippers? I don't have any."

"Then don't wear any," I advised.

Ella couldn't believe her ears. "You mean I should go to the royal ball barefooted?"

"What choice do you have, unless you want to wear those ugly boots you're wearing?"

"And how am I supposed to get to the ball?" she asked. This young woman certainly could think up problems! "The royal palace is almost a mile from my house."

I knew Ella wouldn't like my answer. "I suppose you'll just have to walk."

A big frown appeared on her face. This wasn't the kind of help she had hoped to get from her fairy godmother. "But they'll never let me in if I don't arrive in a fancy, horse-drawn carriage," she whined.

"You're right," I agreed. "They may not let you in through the main gate, but I don't think there's anyone guarding the door to the kitchen. Do you?"

"I guess not," she said tentatively. "At least I hope not!"

Ella seemed uncomfortable with my answers. She'd

never done anything quite so daring before. I wasn't surprised when I heard another "but."

"But if a prince asks me to dance, what should I say?"

"Ask him to be careful not to step on your toes," I joked.

Ella laughed so hard, she had to use the handkerchief again. Sensing she was close to deciding in favor of going to the ball, I gave her one more push. "What have you got to lose?"

"Nothing!" Ella exclaimed, smiling from ear to ear. "Nothing at all!"

She stood up to shake my hand. "Thank you for all your help. I've got to go now. I've got so many things to do!"

Before she left, I offered her some final advice. "If you don't want your stepmother and stepsisters to know you've been to the ball, be sure to leave by twelve o'clock sharp. That way you'll be back in bed by the time they get home."

I was quite pleased with myself for helping Ella. Relaxing for a moment with a glass of lemonade, I wondered if the fairy godmother with all her magic could have done a better job. I spent a good part of the day congratulating myself and feeling thankful I'd gotten through my first problem without messing up.

After dinner, I was surprised by a knock at the door. When I opened it, I discovered a distinguished-looking elderly gentleman. He looked ever-so-much like the king, as pictured on every postage stamp in Bavaria, except that this man looked older, frailer, and far more worried. He must have been trying to keep his visit a secret; no guards or footmen were with him. I curtsied deeply as soon as I let him in.

"Enough of that," he blustered. "I must see the fairy godmother at once!"

"I'm sorry, Your Highness," I explained. "She's away. Can I help you?"

"Perhaps," he replied. "Do you know where she keeps her magic potions?"

"If you tell me which potion you'd like, I'll be happy to look," I said in as helpful a voice as I could muster.

The king looked embarrassed. "Well, actually, I'm looking for a potion that would enable me to, well…live forever."

I offered the king a comfortable chair, excused myself, and went to the cabinet where the fairy godmother kept her potions. In a short time I returned with a handful of bottles. "I've found a potion to keep your breath fresh longer, and one to make your suntan last longer. But I can't find anything to help you live longer, not even for a day."

His royal highness was definitely not overjoyed by this news. "In that case, I'll wait here till the fairy godmother returns. You see, I'm not feeling well, and the royal doctors haven't been much use."

"I'm sorry to hear that, Your Highness. What seems to be the problem?"

"My back, for one thing. It's killing me. And I can't sleep at night because of terrible gas pains, not to mention splitting headaches. My eyesight's growing dim. I'm deaf in one ear. I'm growing forgetful…or did I mention that already? But worst of all, my twin sons are driving me crazy! Aside from that, I'm fine—just fine." There was no mistaking his sarcastic tone.

"I think you must be terribly uncomfortable, Your Highness. But why would you want to live forever? Surely your health will continue to get worse as you grow older. In a few years, you'll be confined to bed. Would you enjoy living forever in bed?"

"I never thought of it that way," he admitted thoughtfully. "But at least if I lived forever I wouldn't have to worry about how to divide the kingdom between my sons, Prince Sherman and Prince Herman. They're identical twins, you know. Even I can't tell them apart! You see, no matter how I divide it, one or both of them will be angry with me. Their squabbling is driving me crazy...or did I mention that already?" he asked absent-mindedly.

"Your memory serves you well," I answered diplomatically. "But I wonder, if two sons' squabbling is driving you crazy, how will you like it when you have eight grandchildren arguing over how to divide the kingdom? Or thirty-two great-grandchildren? Or a hundred-and-twenty-eight great-great-grandchildren? If you're not crazy yet, that should do it."

The king appeared lost in thought. "Come to think of it," he answered, "the longer I put off making a decision, the worse it will get. I suppose I'll have to make the best of my situation for as long as I can. You've been more helpful than you can imagine. I'm glad the fairy godmother was away."

With more energy than he'd displayed since he arrived, he got up from his chair and announced, "I must be on my way."

He smiled as though a great burden had been lifted from his back.

He headed for the door, opened it, and was almost gone when he turned and said, "I want you to forget I was ever here...or did I mention that already?"

He reached into his pocket and pulled out a bag of gold coins, which he handed me. He didn't see me collapse into the armchair and pull out a handkerchief to wipe my face. This had been a most unusual day, and I was anxious to relax in a tub full of hot water and bubbles. (I'd found an excellent bubble bath in the fairy godmother's potion cabinet.)

The next morning was uneventful. I'd slept well and was ready for anything. Then, around noon, "anything" happened. Who do you think knocked at the fairy god-mother's door just as I was starting to think about lunch? Prince Sherman and Prince Herman!

The first thing I noticed when I let them in was how angry they looked. They were arguing about something on the doorstep, and they continued to argue as I opened the door.

"I want the horses and the stables so I can play polo," said Prince Sherman. (I could tell he was Sherman because he had a large *S* monogrammed on his tunic.)

"No way," replied Prince Herman. (He was the one with a large *H* monogrammed on his tunic.) "I like to ride, too."

"Excuse me, Your Highnesses," I said as I curtsied. "I'm afraid the fairy godmother isn't here. I'm her assistant."

"That's all right," said Prince Sherman. "Our father, the king, sent us to see you."

I couldn't believe my ears. "He sent you to see me?"

"That's right," said Prince Herman. "You see, he told us he's very sick and doesn't have long to live. And he said we'd have to figure out how to divide up the kingdom ourselves."

"And," Prince Sherman continued, "he said if we couldn't figure it out, to come and see you. Which is why we're here."

"What do you expect me to do?" I asked. "You know, I'm just the fairy godmother's assistant. I don't do magic."

"We know all that," said Prince Herman. "But father said what you do is better than magic."

I was surprised...no, stunned...no, shocked!

"I- I- I'm fl- fl- flattered," I stammered, not knowing what else to say.

"So we'd like you to divide up the kingdom for us," they said in unison.

"I don't suppose I can refuse a royal command," I said hesitantly.

"What do you mean?" asked Prince Sherman suspiciously.

"You see, if I decide how to divide the royal kingdom, then you'll both be mad at me, because I can't possibly make you both happy. But I do have a couple of suggestions."

"Such as?" they demanded.

I cleared my throat to create some drama. "Ahem!"

"Yes?" they asked, waiting for a brilliant pronouncement.

"Well, you could both renounce the throne and let your cousin Fritz rule."

The twins looked at each other, wondering whether the other would seriously consider such a proposal. "Nah!" they said simultaneously.

"Or you could share the throne and rule together."

"Impossible!" exclaimed Prince Sherman.

"Disastrous!" proclaimed Prince Herman.

"We can't agree about anything," added Prince Sherman. He paused, "Well, almost anything. We both agree that's a stupid idea."

"Then there's only one option." Again I paused for dramatic effect. "Prince Sherman, you divide the kingdom as evenly as you can. Prince Herman, you choose which half you want."

Prince Sherman looked at Prince Herman. Prince Herman looked at Prince Sherman. They smiled. Then they looked at me. Still smiling, they both reached into their pockets, pulled out bags of gold coins, and handed them to me at the same time. Then they walked out the door with their arms on each other's shoulders. They barely made it through the door.

"I can't believe it!" I said to no one in particular as soon as I'd collapsed into the armchair again. Thank goodness there were no more visitors that day. I'd had all the excitement I could handle.

That night over dinner, I wondered whether Ella ever went to the royal ball. The next day I found out. Just before noon she knocked on the front door. She was carrying a satchel and looking tired but happy. I was about to ask, "How was the ball?" but she started talking before I could say a word.

"The ball was great! The music! The food! The dancing! Everything! I would never have gone without your help!" she gushed.

"Thanks," I replied. "But I can't take any credit. You did it all yourself. By the way, what's in your satchel?"

"All my belongings," Ella replied. "After attending the royal ball, I really couldn't go back to living with my stepmother and stepsisters. So I decided to move to town and open up a dressmaker's shop. I really am a good seamstress, you know.

"I just came by to thank you and to tell you the latest news from court. Last night, the king announced he was stepping down from the throne so he can travel. He turned the throne over to Prince Herman—all except the stables. Apparently, Prince Sherman has decided to devote himself to polo."

As she was leaving, I said, "I'd like to be your first customer. I'll be in to see you for a fitting next week."

"Thanks," she said. "Maybe we can go to the royal ball together next year."

"I'd love to," I replied. "But next year we'll go in style. We'll rent a coach for the evening. And we'll both wear dancing slippers, too." Ella walked out the door laughing.

The fairy godmother returned the next day. She didn't seem surprised when I told her all the things that had occurred while she was away. "I told you when I left that you could handle whatever came up," she said.

I wonder if those were magic words.

Troop 13 to the Rescue

AN ORIGINAL STORY BY PENNY WARNER

"If we don't beat Troop 7 this year, I'm going to…eat a bat sandwich!" thirteen-year-old Becca Matthews announced to her three best friends as she stepped off the bus at Camp Miwok.

"How about a bat s'more?" CJ Tran planted her small feet in the red dirt of California Gold Country. "Bats taste better with chocolate."

Becca laughed. It had been a long, winding, three-hour drive from San Francisco to Camp Miwok for the scouts' Gold Rush Jamboree. Glad to get off the bus, she took a deep breath of country air—and crinkled her nose. Skunk.

"We came so close to winning the gold medal last year!" Jonnie Jackson said, twisting one of her tight black braids. "We've got to win this year. We've been preparing all month."

Becca imagined the gold medal gleaming against her own fair skin.

"Don't worry; we'll beat Troop 7," replied Sierra Garcia, Troop 13's optimist. "We've chosen our events carefully."

"I hope you're right, Sierra. After what they did to us last year—all those ants in our clothes—I couldn't stand to see them win again." Becca watched the other scouts unloading their gear and preparing their campsites. The competition looked tough, especially fourteen-year-old Tiffany Hewitt, Troop 7's oldest and tallest girl.

"Don't worry, Jonnie," CJ said. "You're so buff this year, you won't have any trouble rappelling into that cavern."

Jonnie shrugged. "I just hope those ropes hold. And what if Tiffany—"

"Scouts!" Susan Sanford called from the campsite. Susan had been Troop 13's leader for two years. The girls admired her businesslike ways and her warm smile—not to mention her tall, athletic build and her gorgeous brown hair.

"Girls!" Susan held up her right hand, the scout sign for quiet. Troop 13 hushed. "It's time to get to work!" Susan's words set everyone in motion. Within two hours, they had pitched their tents, stored their belongings, and lit their evening campfire.

After a meal of hot dogs and s'mores (batless), the girls sang songs and told ghost stories around the campfire. Finally it was time to hit the sleeping bags.

"Flashlights out!" Susan called. One by one the tents grew dark. Within a half-hour, Becca's tentmates were asleep.

But not Becca. She lay awake in her sleeping bag, thinking about the rappelling event that would kick off the Jamboree tomorrow. She wondered if her troop would lose the gold medal to Troop 7 again. After tossing and turning for what seemed like hours, Becca sat up. There was only one way to deal with this excess energy. She switched on her flashlight and rummaged through her backpack.

"CJ! Jonnie! Sierra! Wake up!" Becca whispered.

The three girls moaned and rolled over.

"Do you know what time it is?" Sierra yawned and checked her lighted watch.

Becca nodded. "Yeah, it's payback time." With one hand she held up a plastic baggie full of safety pins. In the other hand was a red marker.

CJ blinked. "What's that stuff for?"

Becca grinned.

Sierra and Jonnie caught on immediately and tossed

back their covers.

"Oh, cool!" CJ giggled as she scrambled after her friends, who were already creeping outside. The four girls tiptoed silently among the tents in the moonlight. The smell of skunk pierced the air. Only an occasional distant howl broke the stillness.

And while Tiffany and her tentmates dreamed about winning the gold medal, the four girls from Troop 13 stood just outside the tent, unfastening the safety pins and uncapping the red marker....

"He-e-elp!"
"Get us out of here!"
"Something's after us!"
"We're trapped!"
Screams coming from one of Troop 7's tents woke the entire camp at dawn. Girls in pajamas, nighties, and long T-shirts scrambled from their sleeping bags to see what was up.

Becca, CJ, Jonnie, and Sierra stayed put, peeking out as everyone else gathered around Tiffany's tent. Even from a distance, they could see the tent shaking as Tiffany and her friends tried to escape.

Through her binoculars Becca admired the red bull's-eye and message on the tent: "Hit the bull's-eye and win a prize!" Several girls were bombarding the target with pine cones that had been stacked conveniently nearby. Becca aimed the binoculars at the tent's door. Safety pins immobilized the three zippers. It took several minutes for the shower of pine cones and the laughter to subside so someone could undo the pins and free the four girls. All four ran for the latrine.

"I guess they had to go!" said Becca, grinning.

"Badly!" CJ agreed.

As the girls dressed for the day, they heard Tiffany yelling, "Those dorks from Troop 13 did this!"

"How'd they know it was us?" CJ whispered. Then she realized they'd been the only ones who hadn't come out to watch the fun.

Jonnie peered out the door flap. "Uh-oh," she said, "here they come."

Four girls from Troop 7 were stalking over. Tiffany wore silky pink pajamas and fluffy slippers. She had tied a sweatshirt around her waist.

Becca stepped out of the tent and stood in her holey "Girls rule!" T-shirt and sweatpants, staring at Tiffany. "What happened?" she asked. "We heard all the screaming—"

Tiffany cut Becca off. "You did that! You and your stupid little pals! Those dumb pine cones woke us up

...and we couldn't get out to use the—to see what was going on!"

"Gosh, that's awful!" Becca said innocently.

Tiffany pulled her sweatshirt tighter around her waist. "You nimrod. We know you were behind it. That prank was just the sort of dorky thing you would do. What if we had an acci—emergency? You know the rules: Any scout who doesn't respect others is not a good scout! Trapping us in our tents is disrespectful!"

Becca tried not to laugh. "You mean like putting ants in people's clothes?"

Tiffany clenched her fists and stepped forward menacingly.

"Girls!" Susan suddenly called out. "Time to make breakfast!"

Tiffany glared at the girls from Troop 13. "We'll get you for this," she hissed. "We'll kick your butts at the rappelling competition, just like we did last year!"

As Tiffany stomped off, Becca stared at the bottom of her sweatshirt. Was that a wet spot?

"Girls! Breakfast!" Susan repeated, eyeing the girls suspiciously. They stifled their giggles and hustled to dress.

Becca thought about the upcoming event as she ate her Eggs in a Muffin. Jonnie was strong and fast, and had done lots of climbing at the gym with her parents. She'd have no trouble rappelling into the 100-foot cavern. But could she beat Tiffany?

"Did you hear about that new scout?" CJ interrupted Becca's thoughts.

Becca shrugged. "Who?"

"Amber something. She's supposed to be some kind of super-athlete. She's been bragging about being a real rock climber, not just a gym rat." CJ pointed out Amber at Troop 10's campsite.

Becca glanced over at the new girl and sized her up quickly. Amber was tall and lanky like Jonnie, with milk-chocolate skin and short, tight curls. It was hard to tell how strong she was under her baggy clothes, but it looked like Tiffany wasn't the only one Jonnie would have to beat.

"Time to go!" Susan called out. The troops hiked down the dirt path to the Haunted Caverns for the rappelling event. At the caverns, the park rangers and troop leaders checked the rappellers' harnesses, ropes, buckles, and helmets, making sure every piece of equipment was in good working order. Finally, Jonnie buckled her fanny pack over her sweatshirt.

"All right, girls," boomed Mrs. Stumplemeyer, Troop 7's leader. "You know the rules, but I'm going to review them." The girls groaned. Mrs. Stumplemeyer held up her right hand, but it was her stern look that hushed everyone.

Becca glanced over the cavern's edge. The steep cliff dropped away into a seemingly bottomless pit. She saw nothing but blackness below and shivered, thankful that this was Jonnie's event.

"When I give the command," Mrs. Stumplemeyer continued, "use your ropes to lower yourselves to the bottom of the cavern within the allotted time. If you're too slow or too fast, you'll be disqualified. We want you to rappel responsibly, not barrel down out of control. The first scout to make it to the bottom within the time window wins this event."

Jonnie nervously checked her watch, then stretched her muscles for the zillionth time. Becca could tell she was anxious to start.

"Hang in there," CJ said, laughing at her pun. "Get it? See you at the bottom."

The girls gave Jonnie a few more encouraging words before descending a spiral staircase to the cavern floor, where they would greet the rappellers with flashlights, cheers, and hugs as they landed.

Climbing down the staircase was almost as exciting as rappelling, Becca thought. The metal structure was shaky and dizzying. When she reached the bottom, she looked up and thought, "I'll bet they could fit the Statue of Liberty in here."

After donning the sweatshirt tied around her waist, Becca lifted her binoculars. She spotted Jonnie between Tiffany and Amber, and she waved the flashlight to signal her support. A hush fell over the crowd as the tiny figures above switched on their helmet lights.

Tweeeet! Mrs. Stumplemeyer's whistle echoed in the cavern.

Ten girls began their descent into the blackness below, guided only by the dim flashlights of their troopmates at the bottom.

"What's happening?" Sierra asked Becca, who was still peering through the binoculars.

"Jonnie's way ahead of everyone." Becca paused. "But that new girl—Amber—she's picking up speed."

Becca shared her binoculars as the rappellers completed the first 50 feet of the descent, creeping down the cliff on their ropes like spiders trailing silk.

Becca took the binoculars from Sierra and focused them on Jonnie. Suddenly she gasped. "Oh no! Amber just passed Jonnie!" Becca's heart thumped. She searched for Tiffany and found her a few feet above Jonnie.

The other girls didn't need binoculars to see what

had happened. Amber had suddenly taken the lead. No one from Troop 13 said anything, but the noise from Troop 10 grew as its members chanted, "Am-ber! Am-ber! Am-ber! Am—"

Suddenly the chanting stopped. The other spectators murmured as they realized something was wrong. Amber had stopped her descent. Becca saw it all up close through her binoculars. "Oh my gosh! Amber's stuck! She seems to be floating in midair."

Sierra took the binoculars and studied Amber. "She's wiggling around…her rope must be caught on something."

Becca retrieved the binoculars and zeroed in on Jonnie, who had almost caught up with Amber. Tiffany was right behind Jonnie. The other rappellers had stopped descending to watch Amber, who was squirming frantically.

Becca trained her binoculars on Amber. "She's definitely caught on something; it looks like a rough ledge sticking out of the cliff. Her rope…," Becca paused, straining to make out what Amber was doing. "She's trying to get free…but every time she wiggles around, the rope rubs against that ledge and…oh no…"

"What?!" CJ shouted.

"…it's…fraying."

A hush fell over the crowd as everyone realized the danger Amber was in. The sharp edge of the jutting ledge was sawing away at her lifeline.

Becca aimed the binoculars at Jonnie again. "Uh-oh."

"What now?" CJ grabbed at the binoculars, but Becca held on.

"Something's wrong with Jonnie now. She's slowing down," Becca said.

"Oh no!" Sierra asked. "Is she stuck, too?"

"I can't tell, but she's definitely stopped." Becca gasped. "She's…trying to reach Amber!"

The three girls looked at each other. "But what about the contest?" CJ said. "Tiffany's almost caught up with her!"

If Jonnie continued her descent now, she would win the rappelling event. But instead she had stopped abruptly. Becca watched through the binoculars as Jonnie began swinging her legs back and forth.

Becca moved her gaze to Tiffany and saw the girl pause for a moment as she reached Jonnie and Amber. Jonnie, still swinging her legs, said something over her shoulder to Tiffany, but Becca couldn't make out the words over the spectators' concerned chatter. Tiffany didn't seem to hear Jonnie either. Or she'd chosen to ignore her. She slid past Jonnie and Amber, continuing her descent.

Tiffany had taken the lead.

The murmuring increased as Troop 7 watched their teammate rappel toward the bottom of the cavern and victory. Becca kept her eyes on Jonnie, who continued swinging her legs, trying to reach Amber. Amber looked terrified as she squirmed around, trying to free herself.

"Oh no!" Becca whispered.

"What?" CJ squealed.

"The rope…another strand is about to—"

The strand broke before Becca could finish her sentence. Amber jerked downward a foot. She screamed, and so did the girls at the bottom of the cavern.

Becca focused on Jonnie. "Come on, Jonnie, come on!" she murmured. Jonnie spent several more seconds kicking her legs as she swung back and forth, trying to gain momentum. Becca could see Amber crying as she reached out for Jonnie, who swung only 2 feet away from her.

With one more vigorous kick, Jonnie was able to grab Amber's outstretched arm. Amber threw her arms around Jonnie like a lost toddler who'd just found her mother.

Gripping Amber with one hand, Jonnie found a foothold on the cliff and struggled out of her sweatshirt. She wrapped it around Amber's waist and her own, tying the sleeves tightly with a knot she'd learned for her camping badge. Then Jonnie opened her fanny pack and pulled out her metal flashlight. She lifted it high in the air and slammed it against the sharp, thin edge of the ledge. Becca watched the rocky tip break off and fall to the ground.

Amber jerked as her rope was freed, but she clung to Jonnie, and the sweatshirt held them tightly together. Together, with one strong rope and one frayed nearly in half, the two girls slowly started to descend.

"She's free!" A cheer went up from the cavern floor. The girls hugged each other, and leaders wiped sweat from their foreheads. Everyone was happy to see that Amber was out of danger. Soon the girls were only 5 or 6 feet from the ground.

And then Amber's rope snapped completely. Jonnie's rope couldn't handle the jolt of extra weight, and the girls plummeted the last few feet.

They landed hard enough to knock the wind out of them. As they gasped and coughed, their troopmates gathered around them and helped them to their feet. It was clear from the cheers that both Amber and Jonnie were going to be all right.

But the members of Troop 7 were cheering for a different reason. Tiffany had landed at the bottom several minutes before Amber and Jonnie. Troop 7 had won the rappelling event.

"Losers!" Tiffany sneered at Troop 13. "I told you we were going to beat you this year!"

Becca shook her head, then turned to help Jonnie remove her gear. Jonnie didn't look so good. "Are you all right?" Becca said as she unhooked one of Jonnie's ropes. "You were amazing!"

"But we lost the event again," Jonnie protested, "thanks to me."

"Jonnie!" CJ said. "You did the right thing. You saved Amber's life. And you risked your life to do it!"

Sierra chimed in, "I thought what you did was great. So what if we didn't win? That's not the point."

"The girls are right, Jonnie," came a voice from the darkness. Susan stepped forward, holding her flashlight. "You're a scout, and that means you help others when they're in trouble. I'm very proud of you." Susan put her arm around Jonnie and gave her a squeeze. Jonnie's look of disappointment faded a little.

Becca glanced over at Tiffany, who was accepting congratulations from her circle of friends. "I just wish Troop 7 hadn't won. They're driving us nuts with all their bragging."

"Scouts! Sco-o-u-uts!" Mrs. Stumplemeyer's shrill voice echoed like a siren in the cavern. "We have our winner! I'm pleased to announce that thanks to Tiffany Hewitt, Troop 7 has won the rappelling event."

A brief spurt of applause followed. It came mostly from Troop 7.

"Yes, Mrs. Stumplemeyer," said another voice in the darkness. It was Mrs. Parker, the leader of Troop 10—Amber's troop. She stepped forward, followed by several other troop leaders. "Troop 7 won the event. But we have another award to present."

"What do you mean, another award?" snapped Mrs. Stumplemeyer. "There's only one winner for the rappelling event. I don't see—"

Mrs. Parker interrupted, "It's great to be a winner. But it's even better to be a good scout—"

Mrs. Stumplemeyer broke in, "What do you mean? My girls are good scouts."

"Mrs. Stumplemeyer, you didn't let me finish. I was about to say that Amber was in serious danger up there, and a scout from another troop forfeited the race to rescue her. This is a stellar demonstration of the Scout Promise, 'To help other people at all times.'"

"So?" said Mrs. Stumplemeyer, puzzled.

"So, while your troop has won the rappelling event," Mrs. Parker continued, "the other troop leaders and I believe that Jonnie Jackson from Troop 13 deserves an even higher honor—one of the highest honors a scout can receive: the Leadership Pin. She clearly gave up her winning edge to help Amber, and she has set a fine example for everyone."

"Yes, but—"

"This type of behavior should be rewarded, not punished. Don't you agree, Mrs. Stumplemeyer?"

Troop 7's leader glanced at her scouts, then nodded weakly.

"Shall we take a vote?" asked Mrs. Parker. "All in favor that Jonnie Jackson from Troop 13 be awarded the Leadership Pin, raise your hands." Ninety percent of the hands went up. "Those opposed?" Several hands from Troop 7 started to go up, then faltered. Only one hand stayed up: Tiffany's.

Tiffany looked around with disgust. "It's not fair!" she whined. "You're just trying to downplay my award by giving her a better one! What about that trick they played on us this morning? That wasn't setting a good example!"

Susan stepped forward and stood face to face with Tiffany. "My girls didn't complain when you put their clothes on an anthill last year."

Tiffany muttered and stomped off. As a crowd gathered around Jonnie to congratulate her, Becca stood back, smiling at Susan. It looked as if one good deed had led to another. Troop 7 may have won the first event, but Troop 13 had won an even higher honor by doing the right thing. Becca glanced over at the girls in Troop 7, who were huddled tightly and whispering.

"I wonder what they're up to," Sierra said to Becca.

"I don't know," Becca replied, "but I think we'd better zip up our tents tight tonight!"

The Clever Daughter

AN ORIGINAL STORY BY MARTHA JOHNSON

The pounding on the courtyard gate came just as Chang Liu's father finished her daily writing lesson. He put the brush down, careful not to spoil the perfect characters on the page, and nodded to Liu.

The gate shook from the fierce pounding. Liu had to fight the urge to run and answer. Instead she folded her hands and walked sedately, as befitted the only child of the head of the village. She opened the gate.

"Master Chang!" The man brushed past Liu as if she wasn't there. "I have a message from the magistrate."

Liu's heart thumped anxiously. The new magistrate was a greedy man, demanding one unfair tax after another from their poor village. What did he want now?

"The magistrate requires one hundred baskets of grain from this village." The man slapped an order on the table. "He will come here tomorrow to collect it."

One hundred baskets of grain! Liu covered her mouth to keep from protesting. If the village lost that much grain, there'd be nothing left in the storehouse for winter. The villagers would starve!

Father knew that—Liu could see it in his eyes. He'd tell the man they couldn't obey the order. Instead, her father bowed. "It will be as the magistrate commands."

When the gate had closed behind their unwelcome visitor, Liu couldn't keep silent. "Father! How could you agree? Why didn't you argue?"

Master Chang frowned. "One does not argue with one higher than oneself. How many times have I told you? At the top is the emperor, followed by the governor, the magistrate, the head of each village, then the men of each village. That is the order of things."

And at the very bottom are the women and children, Liu thought rebelliously. "But, Father..."

"No arguments, Liu." Father rubbed his forehead. "You will go to the storehouse and prepare the baskets. Tomorrow the grain goes to the magistrate."

Liu's stomach knotted with disappointment. How could he just give in? They had to do something!

Her father turned away tiredly, so Liu bowed and left the courtyard. But she wasn't ready to go to the storehouse—not yet. She wandered into the kitchen, where the cook was working on the evening meal. Soon there would be no food left to prepare. Liu's stomach growled as if it knew a hungry time was coming.

Liu watched the cook wrap dough around a bit of meat, preparing it for the pot. As she watched, an idea popped into her head—a daring idea to save the village.

Liu ran toward the storehouse. If her father wouldn't do anything, she would.

By the next day, Liu's father had worried himself sick, so it was easy to talk him into staying in bed. Liu told him she could handle turning over the grain.

When the magistrate and his men arrived, Liu waited outside the storehouse. A group of villagers looked on, and she could hear their murmuring voices.

"Foolish, to let a mere girl deal with the magistrate. As foolish as teaching her to read and write. He'll cheat her, and we'll be left with nothing."

The magistrate stepped forward, and Liu bowed. Her heart pounded loudly. If this didn't work…

"My father is ill," she said. "He has asked me to present the grain." She gestured to the children who had spent hours helping her last night. They began carrying out baskets as the magistrate's clerk counted. Liu cleared her throat. "We beg you, sir, please leave a little grain. Our storehouse is nearly empty."

The magistrate frowned. "Your taxes are required — one hundred baskets." The clerk whispered in his ear, and the magistrate's eyes lit with greed. Liu knew what the clerk was saying: there were not one hundred baskets, but one hundred and ten. She held her breath, waiting for the magistrate to point out her mistake.

He didn't. Instead, he gestured for his men to begin loading. A greedy, satisfied smile crept across his face.

Liu pulled out the receipt she had prepared. "My father directed me to have this receipt signed."

The magistrate gestured for the clerk to bring his writing materials, then he affixed his name and title. In a few moments the wagons were creaking away down the dusty road.

Liu's legs wobbled with relief. The children hurried to pull out the grain that they had hidden away. Master Chang, leaning on the cook's arm, peered into the storehouse just as they finished.

"Daughter, why is the grain still here? I saw the magistrate's carts go by with our baskets."

Liu smiled. "Baskets, yes, Father. Grain, no. The baskets are filled with chaff, with a little grain on top. That way I saved enough to feed the village all winter."

Liu's father went pale with shock. "Foolish girl, what have you done? We were ordered to turn the grain over.

We had no choice but to obey."

Liu's chest hurt at her father's disappointment. "But, Father, I couldn't let the children starve. Besides, I…"

"Enough, enough. I can't listen. When the magistrate discovers this trick, he'll send soldiers to arrest us. We'll be tried before the governor himself."

"Father, my plan will work," Liu protested, but he didn't want to hear. Leaning heavily on the cook, he tottered back toward his room, leaving Liu to listen as the villagers muttered about her.

"Foolish girl, to think she could outwit a man. Now we will all have to pay for her foolishness."

Early the next morning, just as her father predicted, the soldiers came. They hauled Liu and her father off to the city. The villagers trailed along to see what would happen.

When Liu and her father arrived at the city square, the sun was riding high in the sky. The governor sat under the shade of a silken parasol while the magistrate's men lined the baskets up in front of him.

Liu's father bowed to the ground, and Liu did the same. Trembling, she waited for someone to speak.

With an outraged snarl, the magistrate began. "These two have cheated me of my taxes. The baskets this wicked girl gave me were filled with chaff."

He gestured to a soldier, who tipped one of the baskets on its side. A little golden grain spilled out, followed by a pile of chaff. The crowd gasped, and the governor frowned. He turned to Liu's father.

"Well, Master Chang? You are the head of your village. What have you to say for yourself?"

"It was not my father," Liu said quickly. "He was ill, and I gave the magistrate our grain."

The governor frowned at her. "Well? What is your excuse, girl?"

Liu took a deep breath. If she did what she'd planned, she had a chance to save the village. But what would her father think, with his obedience to the proper order of things? Would he ever forgive her?

"Honored governor, may I inspect these baskets?"

He waved his hand, and Liu walked solemnly along the rows of baskets. Then she stopped before him.

"I fear there has been a mistake," she said carefully. "How could these baskets have come from our village? The magistrate had an order for only one hundred baskets from us, and here are one hundred and ten."

The magistrate started to speak, but the governor held up his hand for silence. The governor's clerk began to count the baskets. When he had finished, he nodded. "One hundred and ten."

The governor turned to the magistrate. "How do you explain this?"

"The girl is lying," the magistrate blustered. "She's lying, that's all. I collected these baskets from her village, all right—one hundred and ten of them."

Liu pulled the receipt from her sleeve. "One hundred," she said clearly. "Here is a receipt, signed by the magistrate himself, for one hundred baskets. I'm sure the magistrate would not lie."

"But, but…" The magistrate's stammering was silenced by a wave of the governor's hand.

Everyone waited while the governor examined the receipt and talked with his advisors. Then he turned to the crowd. Liu held her breath. What would he say?

The governor spoke. "Master Chang and his clever daughter are free to go." He turned to the magistrate. "You will give them a bar of silver for their trouble. You will then reside in prison until we can learn how many other villages you have cheated."

The villagers crowded around Liu, and the children hugged her. "How clever she is," the villagers said. "How lucky Master Chang is to have such a clever daughter."

Liu looked anxiously at her father. The villagers' fickle praise meant little to her, and it would mean nothing if her father was still angry with her.

Her father closed his eyes for a moment, thinking deeply. Then he spoke. "At the top is the emperor, followed by the governor, the magistrate, the head man of the village, then the men of the village. That is the proper order of things." Liu's heart sank.

"However," her father continued, "my daughter did not show disrespect for the magistrate. Instead, she allowed him to expose himself as a cheat. So perhaps we should find room for a clever daughter in the proper order of things."

Liu bowed respectfully to her father. But she couldn't hold back a smile.

Liza and the Lost Letter

An Original Story by Bruce Lansky

If you ever go to London to attend a festive royal event, a wedding perhaps, you'll have to wade through throngs of cheering, waving people to catch a glimpse of royalty.

But it's not like that when the royal family is staying in Balmoral Castle, their summer palace nestled in the rolling green hills of the Scottish countryside. There, you often see them riding through town in a horse-drawn carriage, surrounded by a small guard clad in bright red and black.

Every Sunday morning at nine o'clock, the royal family rides past Liza Higgins' house, and Liza is always waiting on the sidewalk in front of her house, waving a little British flag—a one-girl welcoming committee. The first time Liza ever saw the royal carriage, Princess Margaret waved at her. Since then, Liza had come out to watch the royal family ride by every summer Sunday, rain or shine.

One Sunday morning in June, as the royal carriage rolled towards her, Liza noticed that Princess Margaret was reading a letter. Suddenly, the letter flew out of the princess's hand into the air. The carriage jerked to a stop. The guards dismounted and began searching the street.

Liza watched the wind blow the letter into a small alley. She noticed how anxious the princess looked. But the queen seemed impatient. She spoke to the driver, and just as suddenly as the procession had stopped, the guards mounted and the carriage resumed moving down the street.

Liza waited until the carriage and guards were out of sight. Curious, she walked down the cobblestone street to where she had seen the carriage stop. No one else was out on the street yet—most people were still eating breakfast or dressing for church. Liza walked up the alley where she had seen the letter blow.

There, behind a trash barrel, was a handwritten letter on fine stationery imprinted with the seal of the king of France. As she glanced briefly at the letter, Liza noticed that it was written in French. Liza folded the letter carefully and put it in her pocket. She tried to stay calm as she strolled back to her house.

Liza didn't tell a soul about what she had found. All

through breakfast she wondered what to do. If she were the princess, she would want the letter back, unread, and the entire matter kept in the strictest confidence. At church that day, a sermon on the golden rule strengthened Liza's resolve to return the letter as soon as possible.

Once the service was over, Liza told her parents that she wanted to take a walk and set off at a brisk pace for the summer palace, which was about a mile from church.

The gate to the palace was guarded by a gatekeeper who was wearing a tall, bushy, black hat and standing still as a statue.

"Excuse me," said Liza, "but I must see Princess Margaret."

"May I see your pass?" inquired the guard brusquely.

"I don't have a pass," answered Liza.

"I'm sorry. No one can get through the gate without a pass," responded the guard without moving a single body part other than his jaw.

"But you don't understand," insisted Liza. "I've found something that belongs to the princess. I'm sure she'll want it back."

"And, no doubt, you'll be wanting a reward for your service."

"No, I just want to return to the princess what is hers."

"In that case, come back when you have a pass," he said, avoiding her glance.

"But how will I ever get a pass?" asked Liza, who was growing frustrated by the delay.

"I'll be happy to arrange it—for just half the reward," he answered.

Puzzled, Liza asked, "Are you serious?"

Without even looking at Liza, the gatekeeper simply said, "Good day."

Liza didn't move. She was angered by the gatekeeper's greed, but the thought of a reward hadn't even occurred to her. So she reconsidered and said, "Perhaps I will give you half the reward."

For the first time the gatekeeper smiled. He took a piece of paper out of his pocket and signed it. "Here," he said as he opened the gate for Liza and let her in. "Now remember—this pass will cost you half the reward."

"How can I ever forget your kindness?" Liza responded sarcastically.

Another guard escorted Liza to the foyer, where the appointments secretary, who was seated at an ornate wooden desk, was idly turning the pages of a huge appointment book.

"Who is this urchin?" the secretary called out scornfully to the guard.

"Just another beggar looking for a royal reward," answered the guard. "She claims she is returning something to the princess."

"I'm sorry, but Her Majesty's calendar is completely full—for weeks. She has no time to meet with you. But, if you'll just give whatever it is to me, I'll see that it is returned to the princess."

Liza shook her head. "You don't understand, this is a personal matter. I must return it to the princess myself."

"In that case, come back in September and I'll see what I can do. Good day."

"That's ridiculous!" protested Liza. "The royal family will have moved back to Buckingham Palace by then."

Liza did not move. She stared into the eyes of the appointments secretary, so he would know she was serious. "Why don't you ask Princess Margaret if she's lost something. I think you'll find that she will want to see me immediately."

The secretary looked down at his book again. "I'll see. If it's that important, then perhaps I can accommodate you. But you'll have to compensate me for my efforts on your behalf. It will cost you half of your reward."

Liza was quickly learning the ways of the royal court. She spoke through clenched teeth as she controlled her temper, "Agreed." Then she sat down to wait.

In less than five minutes the appointments secretary returned. "You're in luck," he smiled. "The princess will see you. Remember—I get half the reward."

"I have an excellent memory," Liza assured him.

The secretary ushered Liza into Princess Margaret's chamber. As they entered, the princess was pacing the floor. On her face was the same worried expression that Liza had observed when the letter had blown out of her hands.

When Liza entered, the princess paused in her pacing. "Thank you," she said to the appointments secretary. "That will be all." He left, closing the polished mahogany door behind him.

"And who might you be?" Princess Margaret inquired.

"Liza Higgins, Your Majesty," Liza answered as she curtsied politely.

"I am curious to know, what have you found?" the princess asked Liza anxiously.

"A letter, Your Majesty. I believe you lost it on the way to church this morning." Liza retrieved the letter from her jacket pocket as the princess approached her.

Taking the letter that Liza held out for her, the princess opened it. A huge smile covered her face. "Thank

God!" she exclaimed. Then she looked at Liza. "Have you read it?"

"No," said Liza. The princess peered into Liza's eyes to see if she was telling the truth. "You see," Liza continued, "I can't understand a word of French." The princess smiled.

"Have you shown it to anyone?" the princess inquired.

"Not a soul, Your Majesty."

The princess breathed a sigh of relief. "Thank you, Liza. This letter means a great deal to me. Is there anything I can do for you? Name your reward."

Liza took a moment to think before answering. "I did not return your letter for a reward. I was just doing for you what I would have liked someone to do for me. But since you are so kind as to offer a reward, I cannot refuse." She paused, still working out the details of her request.

"However, before I make my request, I wonder if you would summon the palace gatekeeper and your appointments secretary. They both helped me to gain an audience with you. I think they will be happy to know that you have granted me a reward."

"Certainly," said the princess. "Guard!"

Instantly, the door opened and a guard appeared.

Princess Margaret summoned the gatekeeper and her secretary. When they had arrived, she repeated her offer, "Liza, you have done a great service to me by returning a prized possession. How can I reward you? Your wish is my command."

The gatekeeper and the secretary smiled with anticipation.

"Thank you for your generosity, Your Majesty," Liza began. "If you will grant my wish, I humbly request a sentence of two weeks in jail."

The faces of the gatekeeper and the secretary turned white. Their jaws dropped open.

The princess frowned. "I don't understand..."

"You see, although I did not seek a reward, the royal gatekeeper made me promise to give him half of my reward in return for letting me in through the palace gate. And your appointments secretary made me promise to give him half of my reward in return for letting me see you today—even though I told them both that I was here to return something you had lost.

"I hope that you will grant my request, giving half of my reward to the gatekeeper and half to your secretary to fulfill my promise."

"I cannot refuse your request," the princess said, smiling broadly. "Guards, take the prisoners away."

Then, turning to Liza, she said, "Young lady, you have done two great services: one to me personally, and one to the royal family. I have divided the reward for your first service as you requested. But as a reward for your second service—ridding the palace of greed—I would like to give you another reward."

As the princess took a close look at Liza, she said, "You look vaguely familiar. Are you the girl who waves to me every Sunday morning as we drive to church?"

"Yes, Your Majesty. I wait for you every Sunday. Once you even waved to me."

"Well," answered Princess Margaret, "Next Sunday, instead of watching me drive by, how would you like to join me for a ride in the royal carriage—dressed in a brand-new gown?"

"I'd love to!" gasped Liza.

If you had been on Drury Lane that next Sunday morning at nine o'clock, you would have seen Liza, dressed in a beautiful lavender satin gown given to her by Princess Margaret, sitting next to the princess in the royal carriage, waving happily to a huge crowd of friends and family members who had, for the first time anyone can remember, gotten up early on a Sunday morning to cheer Liza and the royal family as they drove by on the way to church.

Keesha and the Rat

AN ORIGINAL STORY BY J. M. KELLY

My name is Keesha, and I am proud to be an African-American girl. I am proud to live in Harlem, and I am proud to be in the fifth grade at Sojourner Truth Elementary School. Did I tell you our school took first place in the New York City Math-Science Tournament? Well, we did, and I was on the team.

I love my mama, I love my baby brother, I love my neighborhood, and I love my friends. But there's one thing I don't love—rats.

Our apartment is kind of small. My mama keeps it clean, but she can't do much about some things. The windows need fixing and the hallways need painting. But the rats are worst of all. I am always worrying: Is a rat going to sneak into my bed? Is a rat going to bite my little brother Raymond?

One time a rat was sneaking along the wall right

toward Raymond's crib. I had to throw a shoe at it—I don't like to get anywhere near rats.

Then I went to Mama and said, "Mama, we have to do something about these rats. They're all over the neighborhood. Why do we have to live with rats?"

"We're poor, Keesha," she said. Mama is a sales clerk at a big store downtown. She doesn't make much money, and she and my dad are divorced.

"I know we're poor, but I don't think that's any kind of reason. I'm writing a letter to the City. I'm telling them they have to get up here and do something."

"You do that, girl," Mama said. "You go right ahead and do it."

And I did it. Then I waited. A letter came back in a fancy envelope that said "City of New York." All right!

I opened it up. It said, "Thank you for your interest." My interest? That's all? Why are they thanking me for my interest? Why aren't they doing something about these rats?

I called up the commissioner of housing. A lady answered the telephone and said, "Can I help you?"

"Rats," I said. "R-A-T-S, rats!"

"We'll send you a form," the lady said. Sure enough, a few days later, the form showed up in our mailbox. I filled it out, told all about the rats, and sent it back. Then

I waited some more. Nothing happened.

"I'm going down there to talk to them," I told Mama.

"Keesha, honey, when you get an idea in your head, you don't give up, do you?" She smiled and I felt good.

Mama went down to the commissioner's office with me. She had to take time off from work, but she was glad to do it.

The woman at the desk told us we had to wait to see the commissioner. So we waited, and waited, and waited. Finally the commissioner came out of his office.

I jumped up. "I want to talk to you. We have rats!"

"I suggest you fill out a form," he said, hurrying out the door. "Or better yet, send a letter."

"But wait a minute," I said. He didn't wait a minute or even a second. He was out the door.

Well! That made me pretty mad. I made up my mind to do something about those rats one way or another.

Then I got lucky. I found out that every once in a while, the mayor visited schools in the city. Guess where he was visiting on Monday? That's right: Harlem— Sojourner Truth Elementary.

I got an idea. I decided to catch a real, live rat and take it to school to show Mr. Mayor just what we had to live with. Maybe he didn't even know how ugly and mean rats were. He had to see these monsters himself. Then he'd want to do something about them.

After church on Sunday I found a white ice-cream pail and poked some air holes in it. I found a board to put on top of it and a stick to prop up the board and a string to tie to the stick. I put some cheese inside the pail and set the trap in the corner of Raymond's and my bedroom where I'd seen the rats.

Now, our apartment has cracks that run along the walls and down along the floor. As I watched one of those cracks, sure enough—I saw a rat. First I saw its nose sniffing around. Then I saw its beady black eyes peering out. Then I watched it squeeze its ugly self right through the crack and creep along the floor.

But I didn't move. That rat was planning on having a nice snack, and I didn't want to scare it off. I could see its yellow teeth and its long, yucky tail. Ugh!

The rat was suspicious at first. It sniffed here and there, its little whiskers twitching. But it couldn't resist and climbed right into the pail to get the cheese. I pulled the string. Bam! I got it.

I didn't want to go near that pail, but I did. I lifted the board a crack and slipped the pail's lid on and tied it down. Then I tied it again, just to make sure old Cheese-Breath couldn't get out.

The next day I took the rat to school. Its constant

scratching gave me shivers up my spine. I would rather have been doing just about anything other than carrying a rat around, believe me. But I was not turning back now.

Our teacher, Mrs. Perez, told us we all had to be really good so we would make a good impression on the mayor. But I thought he should make a good impression on us by doing his job.

Finally, the mayor and a bunch of other people came crowding into our classroom. And who was there with them, big as life? The commissioner of housing. Of course, he didn't even recognize me.

The mayor talked to Mrs. Perez about what we were studying. I was getting nervous. This was the mayor of the whole city. I was just a ten-year-old girl.

He started asking us what we thought about school and all. I knew this was my one chance. I raised my hand.

"Mr. Mayor," I said, "I have something to show you."

He walked over to me, and I took out the pail.

"What's this?" he said. "How nice."

"We have a problem," I said. "In our building . . ."

Was he listening to me? No. He was untying the string and lifting the lid right off the pail.

"Don't do that!" I said.

Too late. As soon as that rat saw daylight, it jumped out of the pail as fast as it could.

Well, you've never seen anything like what happened next. The mayor jumped three feet in the air. All the kids started screaming and climbing up on their chairs. The rat just ran.

Some of the mayor's assistants were yelling. Others were chasing the rat. When they cornered the rat, it turned around and chased them. I had to laugh—I couldn't help it.

Now, old Cheese-Breath wasn't stupid. The rat was looking for a way to get out of there. Finally it jumped up on the window ledge, squeezed through the wire mesh, and was gone.

After a few minutes everybody calmed down a little. "Keesha!" Mrs. Perez said. "What in the world has gotten into you? Why did you play a silly joke like that?"

She was frowning at me, and so was the mayor and all his assistants. I could feel a lump in my throat, but I refused to cry.

"It wasn't a joke," I said. "I wanted the mayor to know how bad the rats are. They are the meanest, dirtiest, ugliest animals in the world. He must not know that, or why would he let them live all over our neighborhood?"

"Where did you get that rat?" the mayor asked.

"In my bedroom."

"You caught that thing in your bedroom?"

"Yes, sir. We just have too many rats."

"And you wanted to show me one so I would understand the problem?"

"That's right. I didn't mean for you to take the lid off the pail. I thought you could peek at the rat if you've never seen one."

"I've seen rats, but not that close." He looked at his assistants and chuckled.

I didn't see what was funny. "We see them that close all the time," I said.

"Okay," the mayor said, "you've made a strong point. And you're lucky, because the man to talk to, our commissioner of housing, is right here."

"I tried talking to him already," I said. I could tell the commissioner was getting a little nervous. "He didn't do a thing but waste my time and my mama's time."

The mayor looked at the commissioner, who shrugged and turned red.

The mayor said, "I'll make a deal with you, Keesha. Exterminators will be at your building by Friday morning. If they aren't, you can phone me directly. I'll tell my secretary to put your call right through. Is that fair?"

"That's fair," I said.

After the mayor left, Mrs. Perez said everything was okay, and that I had done the right thing. "Only . . .

please, Keesha . . . no more rats in the classroom."

"I hope I never see a rat again, Mrs. Perez."

Then all the kids cheered for me.

But I'm waiting for Friday before I start cheering. If those exterminators don't show up, the mayor is going to get an earful, believe me.

Right now, I can't wait to get home and tell Mama everything that happened. She is going to be proud of me. I know it.

Young Maid Marian and Her Amazing, Astounding Pig

AN ORIGINAL STORY BY STEPHEN MOOSER

The Sheriff of Nottingham, a cruel and greedy man, once ruled Sherwood Forest. The Sheriff, who had cold blue eyes and a beard cut sharp as the letter V, had been taxing his subjects so harshly that many of them were now on the verge of losing everything they owned. All across the forest, families were struggling to keep their homes, save their lands, and simply stay alive.

However, even in the worst of times, rays of light do shine through. Sherwood Forest also had such a ray, and her name was Maid Marian. Although she was barely thirteen, her quick wit and wild pranks delighted her many friends and filled the home of her father, Geoffrey the Magistrate, with laughter and love.

One sunny day, when Marian was outside chasing a piglet about the yard, a neighbor, Thomas the Woodsman, came down the road, his shoulders bent beneath the weight of a huge ax.

"Thomas! How are you today?" cried Marian.

Thomas raised up his head and gave Marian a sad, soulful look that described his feelings at that moment.

Thinking that Thomas needed to be cheered up, Marian scooped up the little pig in her arms and skipped across the yard, with her long hair flapping behind her like a golden blanket in the wind.

"Where are you going, my friend?" she asked.

Thomas paused at the gate and regarded Marian sadly with eyes as dark as his tangled beard.

"Have you not heard the terrible news?" he said. "The Sheriff's men are coming to collect yet another tax. If I don't give them half of my wood in payment, they'll take away my cottage and leave my family homeless."

Marian furrowed her brow. "But without that wood, how will you heat your home this winter? And what will you have to sell?"

"That I do not know," said Thomas. He shuffled his feet in the dust and drew in a deep breath. "Without a fire, my family and I could freeze. And without the money I'd make from selling the wood, we can't buy food."

"Ai-yeee!" The piglet in Marian's arms let out a sudden squeal. "Aiyee! Aiyee!"

Marian smiled. "Timothy said that the Sheriff should mind his own business and quit taxing us to death."

Thomas returned Marian's smile. "You have a very wise pig," he said. "How did you ever teach him to talk?"

Marian rubbed her knuckles along the pig's back and he squealed again. "Aiyee! Aiyee!" screeched Timothy.

"Getting him to talk is easy," she said. "Understanding what he says is the hard part."

"You're a very funny girl," said Thomas. He gave Marian a pat on the shoulder. "You and your pig have made me smile for the first time all day." He paused for a moment and looked wistfully off into the distance. "If only your pig really could talk. Perhaps he'd be able to tell me how to save my wood."

"Perhaps he could," said Marian. She narrowed her eyes and put her clever mind into action. "Now, when exactly did you say the tax collectors are coming?"

"The day after tomorrow," said Thomas. "I'm sure they will stop here as well."

"No doubt they will," said Marian. "The Sheriff has been trying for years to drive my father and me from our estate. He wants to take every last gold coin from our pockets."

"Your father has been a fair judge to us all," said Thomas. "I hope the Sheriff never succeeds in driving you from your home."

Marian rubbed her chin and thought. A plan had begun bubbling away in her head, like water in a teakettle. "You know what?" she said. "Maybe my piglet really can save us."

"This is no time for jokes," said Thomas. He wiped his nose with a ragged sleeve. "In two days my family could be in terrible trouble. Perhaps yours will be, too."

"Not if Timothy has anything to say about it," said Marian. She rubbed the pig's back and he let out a long, piercing squeal. "In fact, he just predicted that the Sheriff's men won't get your wood or my father's gold."

Thomas eyed Marian as if she'd suddenly slipped her senses. "Please, Marian, I told you I'm in no mood for joking."

"The Sheriff's tax collectors may be strong, but they are not very smart," said Marian. "Trust me. I have a feeling everything is going to be fine."

Thomas shook his head, waved good-bye halfheartedly, and shuffled off down the road.

"Stop worrying!" shouted Marian as he walked slowly

away, still shaking his head. "Timothy will come to the rescue!"

Thomas raised a hand in farewell but didn't turn around. A few minutes later the woodsman, bent beneath the weight of his giant ax, crested a small hill and was gone.

Marian worked on her plan all the rest of the day. The next morning she hurried to the large stone house of her best friend, a boy named Robin.

"Robin!" she cried, pounding on the heavy wooden door. "I need your help!"

A few minutes later the door swung open and a tall, sandy-haired boy, thin as a wick, came outside rubbing his eyes.

"Good heavens, Marian, do you know what hour it is?" he said, shading his eyes against the morning sun. "I was sound asleep."

"We have no time to waste," said Marian. "I've got a plan and I need your help to carry it out."

Robin rolled his eyes skyward. "Please, not another one of your plans." He shook his head. "Your last scheme nearly cost us our lives. Sneaking into the Sheriff's ball and filling our pockets with fruit for our hungry neighbors was noble, but dangerous."

"And we succeeded, too," said Marian.

"Just barely," said Robin. "I was so weighted down

with apples and pears that the Sheriff's soldiers nearly caught me running away."

Marian looked around and lowered her voice.

"We have to work fast. The tax collectors are coming tomorrow."

"I know," said Robin, nodding. "My father says that if we don't give the Sheriff half of our money, he may try to claim part of our estate."

"If my plan works, he'll have nothing to fear," said Marian. She put a hand on her friend's shoulder. "Can I count on you to help?"

"Help? What kind of help?" asked Robin cautiously.

"I just need you to spread the word about Timothy."

"Timothy? Who's he?"

"My talking pig," said Marian. "He predicts the future too. Sort of."

Robin laughed. "Is this a joke? Pigs don't talk."

Marian tapped her friend on the nose. "I'll explain everything later. Please, I can't do this all by myself." When Robin hesitated, Marian raised two fingers and held them out. "Two forever?"

Robin sighed. "All right, two forever," he said, touching Marian's fingers with the tips of his own.

Two forever. It was a ritual the pair had performed many times. Two forever. That was the deal. When one asked for help, the other always had to agree, quickly and without complaint.

Tax collecting day dawned bright and sunny, but as the Sheriff's tax collectors, Simon and Norman, set out from town in their cart, dark clouds began sweeping in from the west, threatening rain.

At each house along the road, no matter how grand or how humble, Simon and Norman drew up to the door and called the owners to come out.

"By the order of the Sheriff of Nottingham, bring out your taxes and place them in the cart!" cried Simon, who was wearing a tight leather cap ringed by silver spikes.

"Be quick about it or you'll find yourself in the castle dungeon and your home in ashes!" added Norman, who lacked both hair on his head and brains within.

"Here are some of my most valuable possessions," said Christopher the Hunter, carefully placing some of his finest arrows in the back of the cart. "However, I doubt if you will deliver these to the Sheriff. Timothy told me this will be a very unlucky day for you both."

Norman raised his bushy eyebrows. "Timothy? Who is this Timothy?"

"Why, Timothy the Pig, of course. He predicts the future. And quite accurately too. Two days ago he said you would come at precisely this hour, and sure enough, here you are," Christopher said, repeating to the tax collectors the very words Marian had instructed him to say.

"Nonsense," snorted Simon. He snapped the reins and the cart lurched off down the road. "I've never heard such a ridiculous thing. Imagine, a pig that can predict the future."

At each house the story was the same. "Here is my bag of gold," said Mary the Merchant, placing the heavy sack in the back of the cart. "And, Simon, I see you are wearing the hat Timothy predicted you would wear. I'm sure you'd agree he's a very amazing pig."

Simon took off his hat and examined it. "Really? He said I would wear this?"

"With silver spikes around the bottom," Mary said, describing the hat just as she saw it at that moment.

Simon shook his head. "Incredible. I think I'd like to meet this pig."

At the next home, Anne the Seamstress placed a fine velvet cloak with a fur trim into the cart. She looked up at the darkening sky. Any fool could see that rain was coming. "Hurry up. I don't want this cloak to get wet before it gets to the Sheriff. Timothy predicted a storm."

Norman sniffed the air. "I think he's right again," he said. "A storm is coming. Do you think this amazing pig might be able to predict my own future?"

"Of course," said Anne, repeating the words Robin had told her to say. "Anyone can ask him anything."

When the tax collectors stopped at the next home, Thomas the Woodsman quickly appeared, holding an armload of his precious wood. "You can come back for the rest later," he said, placing it into the cart. "Timothy told me that by winter I'd have more wood than I need."

By now the Sheriff's tax collectors could no longer contain their curiosity.

"Tell us, Thomas, where can we find this astounding pig?" asked Simon.

"You'll find him at your very last stop, the home of Maid Marian," said Thomas. He glanced up at the thick clouds. "Hurry now. It's about to rain."

And so, spurred on by the threat of rain and the promise that they'd soon meet Timothy, the astounding pig, the tax collectors hurried to Marian's house.

When they arrived, they found Marian outside with the piglet in her arms and her father by her side. But they did not see Robin hiding behind a nearby tree.

"I have the Sheriff's tax money," said Marian's father. He showed Norman and Simon the coins inside a leather bag. "I'll place it in the back of the cart."

"Do that and be quick about it," ordered Simon. "We must get back before the clouds burst."

"And they soon will," said Marian, for she had already felt a drop. "My pig has predicted a downpour."

Norman raised an eyebrow. "What else has your pig predicted?" he asked, trying not to seem too curious. "Could he tell me my own future, for instance?"

Marian rubbed Timothy's back and the pig went, "Aiyeee!" "He says he knows everything about your future," said Marian.

Norman leaned forward eagerly and so did Simon. "Tell us, little pig, will we find happiness and riches?"

"Perhaps," said Marian, approaching the cart. "Listen carefully to what Timothy has to say." For the next few minutes Marian rubbed Timothy's back, and each time he squealed, she made up something about Simon's and Norman's futures.

All this time, while Simon and Norman greedily followed Marian's words and Timothy's squeals, Robin was removing the goods and gold from the back of the cart. As he took away each item, he substituted it with something else. The bags of gold and coins he replaced with sacks of rocks, the arrows he exchanged for sticks, the wood he traded for twigs, and in place of Anne's fine cloak he put a rag. When he was done, he signaled to Marian and returned to his hiding place behind the tree.

"Timothy has one final prediction," said Marian. She

rubbed her pig's back and he squealed long and loud. "Sadly, he says this will be an unlucky day for you both. In fact, the Sheriff is going to be so displeased with the two of you that he may very well take away your jobs."

"Nonsense," said Simon, shaking his head.

"Flumadiddle!" said Norman. "We are the best tax collectors the Sheriff has ever had."

Marian shrugged her shoulders. "I am only reporting the pig's words," she said. "And he says the Sheriff will not be happy with the worthless things you have collected."

"Now I know your pig doesn't know what he's talking about," said Simon. "Our cart is loaded with all the riches in the land."

Just then, before anyone, including Timothy, could say another word, the clouds split open and the rain began to pour down as though a dam had burst.

"Hurry!" urged Marian. "The road will soon be awash in mud."

"We're on our way!" exclaimed Simon. He snapped the reins and the cart rattled away toward the Sheriff's castle.

Although it rained long and hard, Norman and Simon eventually pulled through the castle gates. As they clattered to a halt in the courtyard, the Sheriff came out to claim his precious taxes.

"What have you brought me?" he asked, stroking his pointed beard. "Show me what you have collected."

"See for yourself," said Norman, who, like Simon, was dripping like a wet rag. "The treasure is all in the back of the cart."

When the Sheriff stuck his head into the back of the cart, he didn't see an ounce of treasure anywhere.

"What is this? Some kind of a joke?" he said, emptying the rocks from a bag. "Don't you know the difference between a stone and a nugget of gold?"

"But...but, sir," blubbered Simon. "I assure you we—"

"And what do you call this?" thundered the Sheriff, holding up the rag.

"A cloak for you?" suggested Norman, wincing. "I don't remember it looking like that when—"

"And what are these?" bellowed the Sheriff, casting the sticks and twigs onto the ground. "You call this treasure? Do you take me for a fool!"

Simon and Norman looked at each other and gasped. "It's just as Timothy the Pig predicted!" exclaimed Simon. "The things we collected are worthless."

"You're fired, both of you!" shouted the Sheriff. He threw up his arms in exasperation. "I've never known such cabbage-headed idiots."

All Norman and Simon could do was shake their

heads in wonder. "Amazing," said Norman. "The pig predicted we'd lose our jobs. And we did. Incredible!"

"I don't know what you two are talking about, but I want you out of my sight forever!"

Before the Sheriff could change his mind and throw them into the dungeon, Norman and Simon hopped off the cart and raced away into the countryside.

"And never come back!" yelled the Sheriff, shaking his fist at the fleeing men. He kicked at the worthless pile of goods at his feet. Ka-blam! His foot rammed right into one of the stones. "Ouch! Ow! Ow!" he roared, hopping up and down on his foot.

As the Sheriff spent the next week in bed, nursing his broken toes, the people of Sherwood Forest retold the story of how Marian and Robin had fooled the tax collectors and saved their precious goods. Everyone agreed that Maid Marian had to be the cleverest soul in all of Sherwood Forest.

But then, even a pig could have told you that.

Dingo Trouble

AN ORIGINAL STORY BY DEBRA TRACY

Australian Words:
Dingo: a wild dog native to Australia.
Station: ranch.
Too right: you bet.
Mum: mom, mother.
Good on ya: good for you.

After breakfast, Samantha and Stephanie sat at their kitchen table, listening intently to their dad. "The police think a pack of dingoes killed our calves," he said. "We lost five of them today." He looked very serious. "Be careful when you're playing, girls. If dingoes are roaming the area, I want you to stay inside. And, to keep you safe, I'll leave Beau behind to protect you."

The twins cheered at this—even two-year-old Mikey happily banged his spoon on the table. Beau was the children's favorite cattle dog. He was playful and gentle, with a handsome white face and a roguish silvery patch around his right eye. He helped round up the cattle on the family's station, which sprawled west of the Great Dividing Range in Australia. Because Beau was a work dog and not a pet, the twins didn't get to play with him too much.

After their dad left, Samantha and Stephanie talked about the wild dogs as they washed the dishes.

"Makes you want to stay inside, doesn't it?" Stephanie said, plopping the dirty dishes into the soapsuds. Foamy bubbles splashed everywhere.

"Too right!" Samantha replied. "But we can't stay in all summer. I'd go crazy!"

"Maybe Dad will teach us to use a rifle, now that we're twelve. Wish we knew how already. Samantha! You're not rinsing all the soap off!"

"Sorry, Stephanie. I was thinking about those dingoes. We'll have to be careful when we go outside." Samantha sighed. Both twins knew that with their mum off visiting her parents, and their dad working, it was up to them to take care of Mikey.

The rest of that morning, Samantha and Stephanie kept Mikey inside the house. They all had fun brushing and playing with Beau. By late afternoon, though, they were bored and decided to risk going outside. First, they scanned the dusty, barren horizon by peering out every window of their ranch-style house.

"I don't see any dingoes," Samantha said. Stephanie agreed. They burst outdoors and spent the rest of the day running with Beau and playing with Mikey on their back yard swing set.

The week passed uneventfully and Samantha and Stephanie forgot all about the wild dingoes.

On the day Mum was due home, Samantha and Stephanie got up early and cleaned the house. Their father smiled when he saw them hard at work. "Your mum's going to be proud of how responsible you two have been with her gone," he said, opening the freezer and taking out some wrapped steaks. "We'll cook these tonight to celebrate her coming home."

Stephanie and Samantha waved good-bye as their dad drove off. When they were finished cleaning, the house looked so good, they decided to stay outside so they wouldn't mess anything up. They took Mikey and Beau and headed for the swing set, as usual. Stephanie helped Mikey climb up the metal ladder to the platform attached to the slide. After playing for a while under the hot sun, Samantha jumped off her swing. "I'm thirsty!" she said. "I'll get us some orange juice."

"Juicy! Juicy!" Mikey called. "Wheeee!" he squealed, zooming down the slide.

Beau bounded playfully after Samantha and trailed her into the house. Samantha was opening the refrigerator when she heard Stephanie screaming and Mikey wailing. Growling, Beau raced to the window and jumped onto the kitchen table to see out. He tore at the screen with his claws, and would have jumped right through it if Samantha hadn't grabbed his neck.

What Samantha saw outside made her heart jump into her throat. Stephanie was standing on the metal slide platform, clutching Mikey to her while three snarling dingoes circled them.

When the dingoes heard Beau barking, they ran to the window and leaped at him, their big paws scratching at the screen. Samantha slammed the window shut. She stood frozen with fear.

"Samantha, help!" Stephanie shrieked.

Samantha didn't know what to do. "Beau, come!" she commanded, pulling him off the table. Beau ran to the back door and clawed at the wood, desperate to get outside. If he had his way and got outside, the dingoes would tear him to pieces. Beau was a strong, loyal dog who would fight to the death to protect his people. But he was no match for three bloodthirsty dingoes.

"I'm sorry, boy!" Samantha said. She ran to the mobile radio in her parents' bedroom.

"Base to mobile one! Come in, Dad! Dad, this is Samantha. Can you hear me?"

"This is Dad," a reassuring voice replied. "What's wrong, Samantha?"

"It's the dingoes, Dad! They've got Stephanie and Mikey trapped on the swing set!"

"I'll be there as soon as I can. But it'll take me thirty-five minutes or so. I'll call the police. You stay inside!" The radio went dead. Dad was on the way.

Samantha ran back to the window. Stephanie was shuffling around on the platform to avoid the dingoes' snapping jaws. She could only imagine how her sister must feel, watching the dingoes' pointed ears, sharp eyes, and bared teeth bobbing in and out of view. The platform on which Mikey and Stephanie were perched was their only hope for safety.

"Hang in there, Stephanie! Dad's on his way!" Samantha yelled, opening the window slightly.

Suddenly, one of the dingoes made a run for the ladder, climbing halfway up before falling backwards to the ground. Stephanie screamed. A second dingo rushed the first and they fought viciously in the dirt. Soon the second dingo backed off. The first one had torn ears and a tawny, shorthaired coat tattooed with battle scars. It was obviously the leader.

The dingoes surrounded Stephanie, jumping at her from three sides, gnashing their yellow teeth. Stephanie had to stand exactly in the middle of the platform to avoid their snapping jaws. Mikey cried in her arms.

"You're doing great, Stephanie," Samantha yelled.

Stephanie didn't answer, but the dingoes ran toward Samantha's voice. They paced back and forth under the window, then bounded back to the swing set. Samantha noticed Stephanie's knees buckling a bit.

Samantha thought frantically. How could she help? She thought about sending Beau outside. He would be killed, but maybe, during the diversion, Stephanie and Mikey could get inside the house.

Beau whined and barked at the door. Samantha couldn't bear to think of losing him. She would let him out only as a last resort.

The dingoes were fighting again. Samantha watched as Stephanie leaned out towards the swings. Was she losing her ballance? She might fall!

"Stephanie! Just stay where you are! Dad's coming!"

But Stephanie seemed determined. With Mikey on her right hip, she leaned over and grabbed the chains of Mikey's baby swing. Stephanie pushed the swing so hard, it looped over the top of the swing set. The swing now dangled further from the ground.

Stephanie sent the swing flying around again and again. Each time the swing wound around the top of the swing set, it rose higher and higher off the ground. Finally, Stephanie looked satisfied. She kissed Mikey's cheek, then took off her sneaker and flung it as far as she could. As the dingoes bolted after the shoe, Stephanie leaned far over the swing set and plopped Mikey into his swing. Stephanie pulled the safety harness down and snapped him securely into his seat. Mikey's legs dangled from the swing, but he was so high off the ground, the dingoes would never reach him.

"Good on ya, Stephanie!" Samantha yelled.

Stephanie's trick infuriated the dingoes. The lead dingo leaped at the ladder again and almost climbed up. Stephanie kicked the dingo, and it fell backward, foam spraying from its mouth.

As Samantha watched, Stephanie swayed slightly. It wasn't even noon yet, but the sun was beating down and the metal swing set was getting hot.

Samantha realized she had to do something. She ran from window to window, scanning the horizon. "Hurry, Dad! Hurry!" But he wasn't in sight. With tears pouring down her cheeks, Samantha walked toward the back door. "I'm sorry, boy. I don't want to do this, but you're our only hope…" She turned the doorknob to let Beau out. Then she suddenly remembered the steaks Dad was going to barbecue for dinner. A plan formed in her head as she let go of the knob. Beau barked a sharp rebuke. "You'll thank me for this later," Samantha said. "If my plan works."

Samantha grabbed a butcher knife and hacked the steak into large chunks. It grew quiet outside and she anxiously peeked out the window. The dingoes were sitting on their haunches, panting. Maybe they were tired out. Maybe they'd just sit there until help came, and Samantha wouldn't have to carry out her plan.

Suddenly, the lead dingo began howling and the other two joined in. They stood up and started circling the swing set again. Stephanie stood calmly in the middle of the platform, staring. Samantha didn't like the way her sister looked. She'd rather Stephanie were crying or screaming—anything but standing dazed like that.

Samantha quickly scooped the steak chunks into a bowl. Taking a deep breath, she walked through the side door that lead to the garage. "Sorry, Beau," she said, shutting the door before he could follow her. Through the garage window, Samantha could see the dingoes, tongues and drool hanging from their mouths. The back door to the house was twenty feet to her right; the swing set about sixty feet straight ahead. She hoped she could reach the door quickly enough. Samantha tried to swallow, but her mouth was so dry that her tongue stuck to the roof of it.

"Here goes…" Samantha murmured.

Samantha dropped a pile of meat onto the cement floor, then opened the back door to the garage. The dingoes were focused on Stephanie and Mikey and didn't see her. She tiptoed across the scrubby grass, dropping chunks of meat the entire way. She was ten feet from the back door to the house when the dingoes saw her.

"Samantha!" Stephanie screamed. "Get inside!"

Samantha ran. She barely felt the ground under her feet as she grabbed the door knob. Samantha heard the dingoes growling a few feet behind her. She jumped inside, slamming the door shut.

Samantha sat down on the kitchen floor with a thud. Beau licked her face and whined with worry.

"I'm okay," she said, hugging Beau. Samantha stood up and walked to the window. The dingoes were eating the meat. She watched as first the pack leader, then the other two dingoes, followed the steak trail into the garage.

Once all three dingoes were in the garage, Samantha cracked open the back door and sneaked across the grass.

When she heard the dingoes chomping on the meat, Samantha ran to the garage door. Slam! She shut the door so hard the whole wall shook.

"I did it!" she yelled. "I shut the dingoes in the garage!" Samantha ran to the slide. "They can't hurt us now, Stephanie!"

Stephanie's legs gave out and the twins sat on the platform together, crying and holding each other. Mikey smiled from the swing.

"What were you thinking all that time?" Samantha asked.

"I don't know," Stephanie said weakly. "Mostly about Mikey, and keeping him safe. Sometimes I couldn't think at all—I was that scared! I also thought about how we were responsible for Mikey. I just knew that I had to save Mikey, so he'd be safe if…if…you know."

Samantha did know, and the girls grew quiet. A few minutes later a police truck pulled up. Right behind it, Dad came roaring up the driveway in his Jeep. Spotting his kids on the swing set, he drove straight to them across the grass.

"The dingoes are trapped in the garage!" Samantha cried. The police ran to the garage.

"Are you okay?" Dad asked.

"Yes," Samantha replied.

They heard three gunshots. The twins looked at each other with relieved smiles on their faces. The dingoes would never bother them again.

Later that evening, after the twins and Mikey had bathed and gotten some rest, Mum's dusty Land Rover pulled into the drive.

"Mum's home!" Samantha and Stephanie shouted excitedly.

Mum burst in the door, and threw her arms around her family. "I missed you!" she said. "Was it too boring with me gone?"

Mum didn't know what to think when her husband, the twins, and even Mikey—who always giggled when someone else did—burst out laughing.

"What? What did I miss?" Mum asked. "And why is everyone dressed up?"

"Samantha and Stephanie are going to receive medals for their bravery tonight," Dad announced proudly. "And you're just in time. We're expecting our ride soon."

"Medals? Bravery?" Mum exclaimed.

But Mum's words were drowned out by the sound of a police helicopter landing in the front yard. She looked at the helicopter, then back at Dad with a per-plexed smile. "Okay, what's going on?" she asked.

"Samantha and Stephanie are heroes, that's all," Dad

answered. "The police and some of the other stations want to honor them. So we're going to town. Come on girls, everyone. You, too, Beau."

"Beau?"

Samantha and Stephanie laughed, and—each taking an arm—led Mum out to the helicopter. "We've had quite a day, Mum! We'll explain it all to you on the way."

Kamala and the Thieves

ADAPTED BY BRUCE LANSKY
FROM AN INDIAN FOLKTALE

Indian Words:

Rupee (pronounced "ROO-pee"): Indian money. One
American dollar is equal to about thirty-five rupees.

Rajah (pronounced "RA-zha"): a title for an Indian ruler
or prince.

If you were a girl raised in a poor village in Punjab,
India, you would probably be married off by your well-
meaning parents to a young man with good prospects.
That's the way it was when Kamala was growing up some
years ago. So that is why Kamala's parents arranged a
marriage with Rajiv, the barber's son.

Kamala complained to her parents. "Who is this
Rajiv? How can you marry me to someone I've never
even met before?"

"Don't worry," Kamala's mother assured her. "Rajiv is a fine boy from a hard-working family. His father owns the busiest barber shop in the village. Rajiv will work there when he gets out of school. He'll take good care of you, and you'll be very happy together. You'll see." And so Kamala's mother proceeded to make arrangements for the marriage.

One day after school, Kamala walked home past the barber shop. It was a hot day, and the door was open. She glanced around the shop and caught a glimpse of Rajiv chatting with a customer. That was the only time she ever saw Rajiv—until, of course, the day of the wedding. But by then it was too late.

Kamala didn't find out until after she was married that Rajiv spent all day at the barber shop joking and playing cards with his friends, not cutting hair. And what little money he made, Rajiv lost at the card table.

Although Kamala kept her home spotless and did what she could to scrimp and save, sometimes Rajiv did not bring home enough money for food. To make ends meet, Kamala did odd jobs for neighbors. She took care of young children and cooked while their mothers carried their laundry down to the river and washed it. Kamala also watched over their belongings to keep them safe from thieves who prowled the neighborhood.

One day Rajiv came home without a rupee in his pocket. "Don't worry, Kamala. I have a plan to get rich. The Rajah's son is getting married and everyone in the village is invited. I will go to the feast and perhaps the Rajah will grant me a favor."

"I hope your plan works, Rajiv. But if it doesn't, I've decided to get a job. You can take care of the cleaning and cooking."

Rajiv protested, but he knew that Kamala was right. So he staked all his hopes on the Rajah. If Kamala took a job, everyone would know that he could not support his family.

At the wedding reception there was a long line of well-wishers, and tables filled with sumptuous food. Rajiv had never seen so much food, so he stuffed himself instead of waiting in line to speak to the Rajah. By the time Rajiv had finished eating, the reception was almost over.

Rajiv approached the Rajah. "Your Excellency," said Rajiv as he bowed, "permit me to congratulate you on this happy occasion."

"Thank you for your kind words," answered the Rajah. "And now, if you'll excuse me, I was just preparing to retire."

Rajiv had not come to the wedding just to flatter the

Rajah. He had come to ask for a favor. If he did not speak up, he would have to go home empty-handed.

Rajiv bowed again. "Your Excellency, I am just a poor barber. I wonder if you'd be so kind as to grant me a small favor on this happy occasion."

A frown creased the brow of the Rajah. He did not know this young man and had no reason to grant him a favor. But to avoid creating an unpleasant scene at the wedding reception, he said, "They say it is bad luck to refuse a request at a wedding, so I will grant you a favor.

"I own some land at the edge of town that is not being cultivated. If you plant it, I will let you keep half of the money you make."

Rajiv bowed low. "Thank you, Excellency, for your generosity." But as he walked home, he was not smiling. Rajiv had been hoping for a few rupees, not a plot of land to farm. Farming was hard work.

When Kamala saw the expression on his face, she sensed the news was bad. "What happened?" she asked. "Didn't the Rajah grant you a favor?"

"I shouldn't have wasted my time," answered Rajiv. "The Rajah was very stingy. He gave me some land to farm for a share of the profits."

"Why are you complaining?" asked Kamala. "Your plan has succeeded!"

"You must be crazy!" snapped Rajiv. "How can I farm without a plow or a bull to pull it?"

"Leave that to me," answered Kamala. "You take care of the cooking and cleaning. I'll take care of the farming."

That day Kamala went out to look at the Rajah's land. It was full of weeds. The soil was good, but hard—it had not been plowed for years. "Maybe Rajiv was right. How will I plow this land?" Kamala wondered. She thought of nothing else all night. The next day she had an idea.

Kamala set out for the land with three children she had in her care. They all carried sticks she had sharpened. As soon as they arrived at the Rajah's land, they began walking around the land, poking their sticks into the ground. People passing by stopped to gape at this strange sight. As a crowd gathered, it attracted some thieves looking for pockets to pick.

When Kamala and the children began to walk back to the village, a thief named Mustapha approached and asked, "Why were you poking the ground with sticks?"

She responded, "It is a secret. I will tell you only if you promise not to tell a soul."

"I promise," said the thief solemnly.

"My husband, Rajiv, was at the Rajah's wedding feast yesterday. The Rajah told him that gold is hidden in this land. I am looking for it."

That night while the village slept, Mustapha and his gang of thieves arrived at the Rajah's land with shovels. They dug up every foot of land looking for the hidden gold. The next morning they were tired and angry at not finding a single coin.

When they saw Kamala approaching, they hid in the forest near the land. They watched as she began to plant seeds in the newly "plowed" soil.

Mustapha left his hiding place and confronted her. "You lied when you said that gold is hidden in the land."

"I didn't lie. There is gold hidden in this land, but to find it, you must plant crops and harvest them." Then, spying several other thieves hiding in the forest, she said, "I see that you lied when you promised you would keep my secret."

Every day Kamala weeded and watered her crop. It was hard work. And when she got home, Rajiv had dinner cooked and ready for her. At the end of the summer, Rajiv helped Kamala harvest the crop and take it to market.

She gave Rajiv half the gold to take to the Rajah, and buried the rest under an apple tree that grew outside her kitchen. She covered the hole with leaves, and leaned a ladder against the tree to make it look as though she had been picking apples. Unfortunately, Rajiv stopped at the barber shop and bragged to his friends about all the gold he had made farming the Rajah's land.

Word quickly got out to Mustapha, who stopped Kamala on the way to the market. "Now that you have found the gold that was hidden in the land, I have come for my share. After all, I dug up the field for you and should be paid for my labor."

Kamala replied, "You dug up the field only because you wanted to steal the gold that was hidden there. I will not pay you a rupee."

But Mustapha did not give up. When Kamala returned from the market, she saw him hiding behind the tree. And when Rajiv returned from delivering the gold to the Rajah that night, he noticed someone lurking in the shadows.

"I hope you have hidden the gold well, Kamala," said Rajiv. "Otherwise the thieves will surely steal it and we will be no better off than we were before."

"Don't worry, Rajiv," Kamala said in a voice loud enough to be heard through the open window. "I have hidden the gold in the tree, where no one would think of looking for it."

Mustapha overheard Kamala and looked up. High in the apple tree, hidden behind dense leaves and fruit, he saw something that looked like a sack. He ran to his hideout and returned shortly with three of his gang.

"Hold the ladder while I go up to get the gold," he commanded. "And be ready when I cut it down." Two men grabbed the ladder, while another stood under the sack, ready to catch it.

Mustapha scampered up the ladder and then from branch to branch until he was close enough to the sack to cut it down with his knife. Not finding any rope, he cut a branch off the tree and hit the sack with it to knock it down.

The sack stayed put, and so Mustapha poked it and heard a buzzing sound. He hit it harder and the buzzing sound got louder. He hit it as hard as he could and knocked it down. And as it fell, angry hornets buzzed out of their nest and swarmed over Mustapha. He started screaming.

"Keep quiet! You'll wake up the neighbors," called the thief who was trying to catch the nest. But in an instant, he heard the buzzing sound and felt the stings of the angry hornets. "Run!" he cried out to the two thieves who were holding the ladder.

But they didn't need any urging. The angry hornets had found them, too. Frantically climbing down the tree with one hand while trying to beat the hornets away with the other, Mustapha put his foot on the ladder, knocking it over—no one was holding it. He had no choice but to jump. He landed on his foot, which buck-led under his weight. Then he hopped after his men who had jumped into the river to elude the stinging hornets.

"Now we're rid of the thieves and the hornets," Kamala said, smiling.

"Very clever of you," admitted Rajiv. "I admire your talent."

"And I admire your talent, Rajiv. You are as good as I am at cooking and cleaning. As long as you stay away from your friends at the barber shop and help me at har-vest time, we just might live happily together after all."

Fishing for Trouble

AN ORIGINAL STORY BY SANDY CUDMORE

"Middle of Nowhere, Mississippi—I can't believe I have to spend my whole spring break here instead of back in L.A.," complained Gabe. "This place is—what—twenty miles from the nearest town? Tunica? What kind of dumb name is Tunica?"

"It's Native American, after the Tunica tribe," said Kayla. She sat in the den with her new—what was he? Her stepcousin? Kayla's favorite uncle, Dan, had recently married Gabe's mom out in California. Gabe was thirteen, same as Kayla. Their age was all they had in common so far.

They'd already gone through Kayla's whole collection of video games. Gabe had easily won them all.

"These games are lame. And you couldn't even get to level two of that last one. I could beat that game when I was ten," Gabe said. "Let's go to an arcade, where they'll have something with a challenge."

"Tunica doesn't have an arcade. You'd have to drive all the way back to Memphis, where you flew in," said Kayla. "We could go skateboarding."

"That's dumb—skateboarding on a bumpy road with no curbs. No thanks," said Gabe. "Back home, I practice on ramps built for competition."

"We could get some worms and go fishing," suggested Kayla. "I have my own fishing boat."

"Right—as if I'm interested in drowning worms in a dinky little lake," Gabe said. "If they teach geography in Tunica, you'll remember that California is on the Pacific Ocean. My dad and I go deep-sea fishing in a trawler."

Why don't you spend your vacation with him, then? Kayla wanted to blurt out. Instead she asked, "So, your dad lives in L.A., too?"

"Yeah. He's on an important business trip. That's why I got stuck here."

If Gabe weren't such a know-it-all, Kayla might almost feel sorry for him. It didn't sound as if his parents had much time for him. Then again, if he acted like this all the time, she could see why they'd ship him off. She stood. "Well, I'm going fishing. You can come if you want to."

Kayla got her tackle box, two fishing rods, two life

It started on the second pull. As they bounced across the choppy waves, the bait can tipped over. Worms crawled all over the bottom of the boat. Kayla scooped them up and shoved them back in the can with both hands.

"Hey, who's driving this thing?" Gabe yelled over the motor's noise.

"Nobody," Kayla said. She leaned over the side to wash her muddy hands.

"Don't you look where you're going?" he asked.

"Why? You see any other boats?"

Gabe looked around. "No. Where is everybody? In California, there'd be two hundred boats out here."

"Not in Mississippi. Maybe ten or twelve boats on a busy day. On a Monday in April, we'll have the whole lake to ourselves," said Kayla. "We just need to keep an eye out for storms. They come up quick this time of year."

The shoreline was covered with cypress trees, tall grasses, and ferns. Kayla turned the boat shoreward and cut the motor. They glided in under the trees. She reached up for a low-hanging branch and stopped the boat by holding on.

Two turtles were sleeping on a cypress root. They looked up, slipped into the water, and disappeared.

"Well, excuse us," Gabe said loudly, as if yelling over the motor.

"Sshh," whispered Kayla. "You'll scare away the fish."

She held the line of one of the rods between her knees, with the hook poking up. Gabe did the same. Then she pulled a worm out of the can. She made a few quick bends in the worm and poked the hook through. After she quietly rinsed her hand in the water, she cast out her line. Gabe picked up a worm and held it near his hook. He tried to poke the hook through it, then put the worm back in the can and dropped his rod to the bottom of the boat.

"So this is how country kids have fun, huh?" he asked.

Kayla ignored him. Her red-and-white bobber ducked under the water. She cranked the reel and pulled out a shiny flapping fish.

"A good-size brim," Kayla said. "Grab it."

She maneuvered the fish up over the boat. Gabe took hold of the line about a foot from the fish. It flopped around and smacked him in the face.

"Yuck," he said. He wiped his face on his sleeve. "This is so dumb. Let's go exploring or something."

Kayla grabbed the fish, pulled the hook free from its mouth, and tossed it back in the lake. It lay stunned on its side for a second, then swam away.

"Okay. We can explore the lake some if you want," Kayla said. "There's an island across from here."

"Move over. I want to drive," said Gabe.

"I guess that'd be all right," she said. "Do you know how to drive a boat?"

"What's to know? If you can do it, I certainly can," he said.

They traded seats, and Gabe drove the boat to the other side of the lake. Kayla pointed to a graceful white heron at the edge of the water.

Gabe shrugged. "Aren't there any Jet Skis on this lake?" he asked.

"Not this time of year," Kayla said. She looked at the sky behind Gabe. "We better get home. Weather's comin'."

"What do you mean?"

"Storm clouds," she said.

"Who's afraid of a black cloud?" Gabe asked.

"Storms come up quick. You don't want to be stuck out on the lake when one hits," Kayla said. "Head toward the silver thing on that shore. It's the roof of our barn. And here—put on your life jacket."

"I don't need a life jacket," Gabe said. He dropped his in the bottom of the boat. They started back across the lake. The sky was abruptly turning dark. The boat rocked in the whitecaps.

"Point the bow into the waves," Kayla called.

"No, I'll go straight. We'll get back quicker," he said

The next wave washed over the side of the boat. They sat in ankle-deep water. When the next wave hit, the boat almost capsized. The engine sputtered and stalled.

"Why didn't you listen to me?" Kayla yelled.

"Well, if you didn't have such a dinky boat!" Gabe shouted over a clap of thunder.

"Let me see if I can get it to start," Kayla called. As they stood up to change seats, rain began to pound them. Another big wave crashed into the boat. Gabe fell, and his face crashed into the bench seat in front. A lot of water had come in. Kayla dumped the worms overboard and started bailing with the coffee can. With her other hand she tugged on the starter rope, but the motor just gurgled.

"It must have gotten swamped when the last wave hit," Kayla called into the wind. She looked at Gabe for the first time since they'd changed seats. He was holding his face, and both his hands were covered with blood. The bridge of his nose was already turning color. Kayla remembered when their mule had kicked her dad in the face and broken his nose. He had looked just like that. Gabe needed to get to a hospital.

Lightning sliced the sky, and thunder crashed around them. Kayla pulled off her shoes, grabbed the rope from the bottom of the boat, and jumped into the water. She knotted the rope to the waist strap of her life jacket and swam toward a small island nearby. When she was able to stand, Kayla towed the boat to shore and pulled it up on the sand. A funnel cloud was moving toward them from across the lake.

"Come on, run!" she yelled. She held Gabe's hand and they ran up the beach to a grassy knoll. At the top a lip jutted out over the beach. Kayla pulled Gabe down. "Stay as flat as you can! Dig in your fingers!"

They pressed their faces into the dirt. The wind pelted them with grit and grass. Hailstones pounded their backs and legs. The wind alternately pushed them against the ground and tried to drag them away. They pressed themselves as low as they could.

Then as suddenly as the storm had come, it was gone, a ghostly blanket blowing away across the lake.

"Your boat's gone," Gabe said when he looked at the empty shore below.

Kayla looked down the shoreline. The aluminum boat was smashed on some large rocks. Trees were pulled out and branches were everywhere.

"What the heck was that?" Gabe said.

"They don't teach you about tornadoes in California?" Kayla asked.

She found her tackle box on the rocks near her wrecked boat. She used her pocketknife to cut off a section of her pants leg, then soaked the denim in the lake.

"Lean against the bank," Kayla said. She pressed the roll of denim against Gabe's bleeding nose. He winced at the pressure. Next she made a horizontal slice in her T-shirt. She tugged, and the bottom third of her shirt ripped away. She shivered. Higher up the bank, Kayla saw a paddle from her boat. She got it and tied the strip of fabric from her shirt onto one end of the paddle.

"Mom will be watching for us," she said. She stood next to Gabe and waved her T-shirt flag high in the air.

Gabe took the compress away from his nose.

"If it weren't for you, I'd be dead out there in the lake," he said. His nose dribbled two streams of blood.

"You better put that back on your nose," Kayla said. She kept waving her flag.

"I'm serious, Kayla. I had no idea what to do," he said.

"Hey, look over there across the lake!" Kayla exclaimed. "That's our ski boat heading this way. My mom and dad must have seen the flag." She waved the flag to let her parents know she saw them. "I'm glad the tornado didn't wreck our ski boat. Who knows . . . you might have to come back here in the summer."

"I'd like that," Gabe said quietly. "Would you teach me how to ski?"

"Oh sure," Kayla said. "You want me, a dumb country girl, to teach you something?"

"I'm sorry," Gabe said. "I know I was a real jerk."

"Come on." Kayla helped Gabe up, and they walked down the bank to wait for the boat.

"I mean it," Gabe insisted. "You really saved my life. And you know how to do more stuff than any of my friends at home. Like putting a worm on a hook—I didn't know how to do that." Blood ran down and dropped off his lip.

"Well, I guess I know a lot of stuff about Mississippi," Kayla said thoughtfully. "But I'd be pretty lost in L.A.— you'd be the expert on that!"

"You'd do fine," Gabe told her. "Maybe sometime you could come out and visit. I'd show you around."

Kayla looked at him. "That would be fun." Then she smiled. "I guess you aren't such a big jerk after all."

"Yah . . . well," Gabe mumbled, embarrassed. "I just want us to be friends."

"Friends it is, then," said Kayla. She reached out her hand.

Gabe smiled with relief. "Friends," he said as he reached out to take Kayla's hand.

Grandma Rosa's Bowl

ADAPTED BY BRUCE LANSKY
FROM A GRIMM BROTHERS' STORY

While visiting a poor village in Mexico, I stopped in an antique shop and picked up a dusty old diary.

The shopkeeper told me that it had belonged to a girl named Maria, who had lived nearby with her mother, Sevilla, many years ago. I hope she will not mind if I share her story with you.

Maria's father had died when she was young, so her mother worked very hard as a potter to make a modest living. When Maria's father's mother became too old and frail to take care of herself, she had no alternative but to move into the little house of Maria and her mother.

From the very first day, Maria enjoyed Grandma Rosa's company. While Sevilla worked at the potter's wheel, Grandma Rosa made herself useful by mending clothes. But because her eyes were weak and her hands trembled, putting the thread through the tiny eye of the needle was very hard for her. So Maria helped her grandmother thread the needle and was rewarded with fascinating stories about her father when he was a boy.

Sevilla was worried about making ends meet now that there was one more mouth to feed. The first night at the dinner table, when Grandma Rosa spilled some soup, Sevilla got angry. "You should be more careful," she warned. "I work hard to put food on the table."

The next night, when Grandma Rosa dropped a dinner bowl on the floor, Sevilla became even angrier. "That beautiful dinner bowl would have brought ten pesos in the market. Now it is broken. You are too clumsy to eat from my best pottery. Here is a plain clay bowl. Eat from that."

The very next night at dinner when Grandma Rosa spilled her coffee on the rug, Sevilla lost her temper. "*¡Ay, caramba!*" she yelled. "First you waste my good soup, then you break my beautiful bowl, and now you stain my carpet. You are too clumsy to eat with us in the dining room." Sevilla set up a little table on the front porch, where Grandma Rosa finished her dinner.

After dinner Grandma Rosa went to her room with her head hanging down. When the old woman was getting ready to go to sleep, Maria came to her bedside to comfort her. The girl whispered to her grandmother,

"I'm very sorry about the way my mother treated you. I know your feelings are hurt. I've thought of a way to help you: Tomorrow night at dinner, I want you to drop your bowl again."

"I do not understand," answered Grandma Rosa in a low voice. "If I drop my bowl, your mother will get upset and yell at me again."

"She may get angry, but don't worry," whispered Maria. "Everything will work out. You'll see."

The following night at dinner, Maria and Sevilla heard a loud crash on the porch. When Sevilla rushed out to see what had happened, she found that Grandma Rosa had dropped her clay bowl, and it had broken into several pieces.

"You are so clumsy!" she scolded. "Pick up the pieces and glue them back together. I'm not giving you another bowl to break."

Grandma Rosa's eyes filled with tears. Maria helped her grandmother up from the table and guided the frail woman to her room.

Then Maria returned to the porch and picked up the pieces of the broken bowl.

Later on that evening, Sevilla found Maria gluing the pieces of Grandma Rosa's broken bowl together. "How nice of you to fix Grandmother's bowl for her," Sevilla said.

"You are mistaken, Mama," answered Maria. "Tomorrow I am going to make a beautiful dinner bowl for Grandma Rosa. This glued-together bowl I will save. Many years from now, when you are as old and frail as Grandma Rosa, I will give it to you."

Now Sevilla's eyes filled with tears. She wept because she felt ashamed of the way she had treated her mother-in-law. And she wept because she was proud of Maria for having the wisdom and the courage to show her the error of her ways.

As soon as Sevilla's tears had dried, she went to Grandma Rosa and begged to be forgiven.

The next day, when dinner was served, Grandma Rosa was again seated at the dinner table. Unfortunately, while stirring sugar into her coffee, she knocked the sugar bowl onto the floor.

Sevilla looked down at the broken sugar bowl. She looked at the sugar that had spilled on the floor. Then she looked at Grandma Rosa and smiled. "Don't worry, Mama. Accidents sometimes happen. Enjoy your dinner."

And that was the first of many happy meals Maria's family enjoyed together from that time forward.

Railroad Through and Through

An Original Story by Cynthia Mercati (Based on a True Story)

Kate Shelley loved the railroad more than anything. She loved the thrill of adventure she felt at the very sight of the burly trains. She loved listening to them roar past her family's Iowa farmhouse, some heading east toward Chicago, some bound west, toward the big Des Moines River Bridge and beyond. She loved wondering about the passengers and imagining their destinations.

Once, the railroad had sustained the Shelley family. Kate's father had worked on the Chicago and Northwestern Railway. Every morning he'd headed off to work, whistling happily but off-key, his sinewy muscles dancing under his flannel shirt. He'd loved his job as a section foreman, and like Kate, he'd loved the trains that zipped across Iowa's prairies.

But her father was gone now. Three years earlier, he'd

been killed in a railroad accident.

"Your father died as he would have wanted: working on the rails," Mrs. Shelley had told her children.

Now the family depended on their tiny farm, which was no more than a patch of pasture tucked in the rolling bluffs between the Des Moines River and Honey Creek. As the oldest child, fifteen-year-old Kate had many responsibilities. She was in charge of the vegetable garden, she helped with the plowing and planting, she gathered firewood, and she cared for her younger siblings. The whole family worked long, hard hours. But at the end of every month, they still struggled to pay the bank what they owed on the farm.

Still, they managed to get by. At night, as Mrs. Shelley mended clothes and the children sat in front of the fire, they often talked wistfully about the happy times that had gone before, when their father was alive.

But on this night, July 6, 1881, the younger children were asleep, and Mrs. Shelley was sewing. Kate sat by the window, watching as lightning lit up the sky and rain fell in heavy sheets.

Suddenly, Kate called out. "Ma, look!" As Mrs. Shelley rushed to her daughter's side, Kate pointed out the window. "Honey Creek's over its banks. It's rising faster than I've ever seen!"

Mrs. Shelley laid a reassuring hand on Kate's shoulder. "Don't worry. We've been through storms before."

Mrs. Shelley returned to her sewing, but Kate was fixed at the window. The Shelleys' little farmhouse nestled right beside a small bluff that led up to the Honey Creek railroad bridge. Many times Kate had clambered up that bluff to look down at the usually friendly water. Tonight, Honey Creek looked like a witch's cauldron, bubbling and boiling.

"We have been through storms before," Kate thought, "but we've never been through one like this!"

The driving wind squealed through the loose chinks in the cabin wall, and the rain continued falling in torrents. Suddenly, the shrill whistle of a train pierced through the thunder.

"Sounds like a pusher engine," Kate told her mother. "I recognize its whistle." A pusher engine was one of the locomotives that sat by the side of the tracks until they were needed to help push or pull trains up a slope.

"Railroad men!" Mrs. Shelley said with fond exasperation. "Who else would be out on a night like this!" She shook her head and looked at Kate. Each knew the other was thinking of Kate's father. "I'm railroad through and through!" he'd loved to boast. "If I have to get a train somewhere, nothing can stop me!"

The engine's bell clanged twice—and then a new noise crashed through the night. It was the sound of shattering timbers, followed by men screaming.

"The bridge!" Mrs. Shelley exclaimed. "The Honey Creek Bridge must have collapsed!"

Without a word, Kate dashed for the door. She yanked on her heavy boots and grabbed her coat from its peg. Her mother was right behind her, pulling her back. "Where do you think you're going?"

Kate jerked on her scarf and tied it under her chin. "To help those men!"

"Kate, you can't go out in this!" Mrs. Shelley gestured helplessly toward the door. "If only your pa were here—he'd know what to do!"

"If Pa were here, he'd be out that door in a flash!"

Mrs. Shelley shook her head. "Kate, there's a big difference between what a man can do and what a fifteen-year-old girl can do!"

Kate's head went up, and her chin—clefted and strong, just like her father's chin—was set stubbornly. "Pa was railroad through and through—and so am I!" Her eyes flashed. "I've got to do what I can!"

Mrs. Shelley looked at Kate for a moment, then reached for the small lantern that hung by the door. She handed it to her daughter. Tenderly, she pulled the collar of Kate's coat close around her throat.

"Be careful," she said softly, "and come home safe. I couldn't bear to lose you, too."

"Don't worry, Ma," Kate said, then she headed outside. The wind and rain pummeled her like a prizefighter. Gasping for breath, she fell back against the door. "Maybe Ma was right," she thought. "Maybe this isn't a night for a girl to be out!" But she gathered her courage, held her lantern high, and struck out.

She waded through the flooded front yard and turned onto the path that led up the bluff. Kate had to fight the wind and rain to keep her balance. She was out of breath when she reached the crest of the hill.

Just a few minutes ago, a sturdy wooden trestle had spanned the creek. Now all that remained of the Honey Creek Bridge were some ragged timbers. A small section of the pusher engine jutted out of the water. Frantically, Kate waved her lantern back and forth, trying to signal the men whose cries she'd heard earlier. Almost immediately a gust of wind blew out the puny light. But the men had already seen it.

"Hullo!" they shouted.

Kate set down her now-useless lantern and cupped her hands around her mouth. "How can I help you?"

"We're all right!" one of the men shouted back at her.

"It's the people on the Midnight Express you've got to help!" He paused to draw a breath. "I'm the engineer and this is my brakeman. We had orders to take the engine out and look for trouble—and we sure found it! The Midnight Express will be headin' right this way, and it won't know anything 'bout the bridge collapsin'!" He coughed from the strain of shouting over the storm. "It'll smack into the water—with hundreds of people on board!"

"Don't worry!" Kate shouted back. "I'll get word to it!" Then, suddenly, she wondered—how was she going to do that on a night like tonight?

Maybe she could go home, relight her lantern, climb back up the hill, and flag down the train as it approached. No, that was no good. Even if the lantern didn't blow out again, the engineer would never spot its feeble light in this storm. There had to be another way.

Kate stood stock-still, mentally scanning all the things her father had told her about how the railroad worked. "How were the stations alerted to impending danger?" she wondered. "Of course! By telegraph!"

Moingona was the nearest railroad station. If she could make it there, she could tell the telegraph operator about the collapse of the bridge, and he could send her message crackling eastward through the wires. The

Midnight Express could be stopped at one of the stations before Honey Creek. She had to get to Moingona as quickly as possible.

If she hitched up the horse and rode to the station, she'd have to take the road that wound through the bluffs, and that would take far too long. Even now the Midnight Express might be starting out. The only other way to reach Moingona Station would be to follow the tracks to the big Des Moines River railroad bridge, and then cross the bridge. The station was on the other side.

The Des Moines River Bridge was a ladder of wooden crossties about two feet apart stretching nearly seven hundred feet across the water. It was hard to walk the bridge even in good weather, and people seldom attempted it. To try crossing it tonight, in the midst of this terrible storm, would be very dangerous. A shiver of fear shot down Kate's spine. Could she do it?

Kate drew a deep breath. It wasn't a question of whether she could do it—she had to do it. "Hundreds of people," she thought, "and I'm the only one who can save them."

Kate turned and started along the tracks, head down against the wind and pelting rain. When she reached the slope that led to the Des Moines River Bridge, she stood for a moment, staring up. Only now did she realize how much steeper it was than the little hill she'd climbed to reach the Honey Creek Bridge. She mustered all her determination, then bent almost double and half-crawling, Kate fought her way up. Finally, she reached the top—and the big bridge.

Panting, Kate peered through the rain, straining to see the other bank. But she couldn't. The bridge seemed to stretch away until it was swallowed up in blackness. If she tried to cross, would she, too, be swallowed up?

Kate tossed her head, trying to shake away her fear. "You're just dawdling, Kate Shelley," she chided herself. "Now get going!"

By now the storm was so fierce, she could barely stand up. How could she keep her balance stepping from wooden tie to wooden tie? She couldn't. "I'll have to crawl," she whispered to herself. "It's the only way."

Kate dropped to her knees. Normally, the bridge rose high above the river, but now the angry water seemed to be churning just below her. One wrong move, one slight slip, would plunge her down into it. With the wind and rain tearing at her, Kate started inching forward.

With only lightning flashes to show the way, Kate relied on touch to guide her. She would reach out one hand to find the next tie, then crawl over it. Reach out, crawl over. Inch by dogged inch, Kate made her way forward. Reach out, crawl over. Again and again. Kate cut her hands and legs on the twisted spikes and nails that studded the ties; her face was numb with cold. But she kept going. The river raged below her, splattering her with foam.

Reach out, crawl over. How far had she come? How much farther did she have to go? She had no way of knowing. She only knew that she had to keep going. Reach out, crawl over. Reach out—nothing there!

One of the ties was missing.

Screaming, Kate fell forward. Her right hand shot out, and she grabbed the iron rail. She was dangling over the river now, feet flailing the air. Gasping and half crying, she pulled her other arm up to grip the rail with both hands. The wind yanked the scarf off her head. She saw it swirl helplessly in the wind, then disappear. Would she, too, disappear into the storm?

Kate tightened her grip, wincing with the effort. With more strength than she'd known she possessed, she pulled herself up until she was again kneeling on one of the wooden crossties.

Breathing in violent jerks, Kate huddled on the bridge. Her heart was beating so hard, she could hear it. She was dizzy; her stomach was churning. She had almost fallen. If she went on, she would surely fall!

How would it feel to plunge into that rushing river? How long would it take for the current to squeeze the breath out of her lungs? Kate willed her heart to slow. She swallowed, took a deep breath, then took another. She knew she had to fight down her panic, or she'd be lost— and with her, the only hope of hundreds of people.

"I can do it," she muttered in jerky bursts. "I can!"

Kate gritted her teeth. Tie by tie she was going to conquer this bridge! She had to. Reach out, crawl over. Her muscles were cramped and aching, and her eyes stung with tears against the cold. When she finally reached the end of the bridge and stood, her legs trembled, exhausted. But she couldn't afford to rest. Moingona Station was still a half-mile away. Kate started running down the tracks, slipping on the wet ties again and again, then struggling to her feet. But she didn't stop; she couldn't. Finally, she saw the faint lights of the railway station beckoning her.

The telegraph operator and several other railroad men were seated inside the station around a pot-bellied stove, hands outstretched. As Kate crashed into the room, their heads jerked around. Her red hair was plastered to her head, and she was gasping for air

"The Honey Creek bridge!" Kate rasped at the startled men. "It's collapsed!

The operator jumped to his feet. "Are you sure about that?"

Kate nodded. "I'm Kate Shelley; our farmhouse is right next to the bridge! You've got to warn the Midnight Express!"

Without another word, the telegraph operator ran to his desk. Kate sagged onto one of the wooden benches that ringed the room. She was dazed with exhaustion; still, she smiled as she heard the urgent tapping of her message across the telegraph wires.

But had her warning come in time?

The other men gathered around the telegraph desk, waiting for the reply. Kate stayed on the bench. The only sounds to be heard in the room were the hissing stove, the roaring storm, Kate's ragged breathing, and the ticking of the clock.

Then they heard a reply being tapped back. Quickly, the operator translated. "The Midnight Express has been warned and halted. Everyone's safe!"

The men cheered, but Kate Shelley was not finished yet. She forced herself to stand on her wobbly legs. "The pusher engine—the engineer and his brakeman—they're stranded in Honey Creek!"

"We'll send out a rescue party," the operator said. He surveyed the bedraggled girl. "But you'd better stay put.

You've done enough for one night."

Kate wouldn't be put off. "Your party would have trouble finding them in the dark. I know exactly where they are. I promised myself I'd help those men, and I'm not going to quit now!"

Quickly, the railroad men climbed aboard an engine sidetracked in the Moingona Station yard. Several of the men rode atop the engine. Kate, wrapped in a blanket, sat in the cab. The engine pulled away from the station and headed onto the Des Moines River Bridge.

The engine stopped well before Honey Creek. Quickly, Kate led the railroad men to the crest of the bluff, where they could see the engineer and brakeman in the water, still clinging to the wrecked pusher engine. As she watched, thick ropes were lowered into the water and the stranded men grabbed on gratefully. Slowly, they were hauled out of the creek. Only when Kate saw that the two men were safe on the bank did she allow one of the rescuers to lead her down the hill and home.

Alerted by the noise of the rescue, Mrs. Shelley was standing at the door of the farmhouse. When she saw a lantern swinging through the darkness, Mrs. Shelley ran down the path and gathered her daughter in her arms. "Kate," she breathed, "tell me that you're all right!"

Bone-weary and shivering uncontrollably, Kate

smiled. "I'm fine, Ma," she said, "only a little cold."

Mrs. Shelley led Kate into the cabin, and the railroad man followed them. "You don't know how worried I was, Kate," her mother murmured. Now Margaret, Mayme, and John came running into the kitchen. They mobbed Kate, tugging at her coat and demanding answers, all of them talking at once.

"She's a brave girl, your daughter," the railroad man told Mrs. Shelley above the babble. "I still can't quite believe what she did tonight!"

"I can!" Mrs. Shelley said quickly. Her eyes sparkled with tears of relief, and one arm was wrapped firmly around Kate. "Kate is railroad through and through!" Mrs. Shelley said. She pressed her lips against Kate's wet hair, whispered, "You did all of us proud tonight, Kate—but especially your pa. You did just what he would have done! Tonight there was another Shelley working on the rails."

In recognition of Kate's heroism, The Chicago Tribune paid off the mortgage on the Shelley farm. In addition, a bridge across the Des Moines River was named in her honor. It's called the Kate Shelley High Bridge, and it crosses the river not far from the site of Kate's big adventure.

Sarah's Pickle Jar

ADAPTED BY BRUCE LANSKY
FROM A CHINESE FOLKTALE

Polish Word:

Zloty (pronounced "ZLO-tee"): Polish money. One American
dollar is equal to about three zlotys.

Yiddish Word:

Oy gevalt (pronounced "oee ge-VALT"): Oh, my goodness.

On Monday business was very slow for Izzy the Tailor.
He worked in the back room of a clothing shop in Chelm,
a village in Poland too small to appear on any map. Not
a single customer had come in all day, so by four o'clock
Izzy decided to leave work early. After all, what is the
point of staying at work if there's nothing to do?

As he walked through town, Izzy lingered at a bakery
window. He wanted to buy some pastries, but he hadn't
made a single *zloty* all day.

Izzy was hungry, and the sight of so many good things to eat led him into the bakery. He stood in front of the glass counter, which was filled with apple strudels, poppy-seed cakes, and cheese Danishes that, believe me, are to die for.

As he gazed at the pastries, Izzy took a deep breath and sighed. A smile replaced the sad expression that had been on his face. The smell of the pastries was so divine, Izzy thought for a moment that he had died and gone to heaven.

"Good afternoon, Izzy," said Jacob the Baker. "What can I do for you? A piece of fresh-baked apple strudel, perhaps?"

"Just looking," said Izzy.

Now business had been slow at the bakery, too, and Jacob had a lot of unsold pastries that were growing staler by the hour. So his mood had grown increasingly sour as the day went on.

"Just looking, my foot!" said the frustrated baker. "You're also smelling. And smelling will cost you a zloty."

Izzy looked at the baker incredulously. "You must be kidding!"

"You are standing in my bakery, filling up your nose with the smell of my pastries. Pay me the zloty and be on your way."

"I'm sorry, but I don't have a zloty in my pocket. If I did, I would have bought a piece of strudel," Izzy explained.

"Whether you fill up on the smell of strudel or the taste of strudel, it's all the same to me. I'll see you in court tomorrow morning!" the baker barked.

When Izzy got home he did not greet his wife, Rivka, with a kiss as he usually did. He did not greet his daughter, Sarah, with a hug as he usually did. Instead, he slumped in his armchair and stared into space.

"What happened to my kiss?" asked Rivka.

"What happened to my hug?" asked Sarah.

Izzy groaned, "Did I have a bad day?" Although it sounded like a question, Rivka and Sarah knew that it was the answer.

"Tell me what happened," asked Sarah.

"You don't want to know," replied Izzy, rolling his eyes. Then he told his sad story.

"*Oy gevalt!* Do you have problems!" exclaimed Rivka.

"Don't worry, Father. I'll think of something," said Sarah. She put her arms around his neck and gave him a hug. Then she went off to bed.

The next morning Sarah refused to go to school. Over her mother's objections, she went to court with Izzy. Eyes downcast, Izzy shuffled along slowly, trying to delay the inevitable. Sarah eagerly pulled her father forward with one hand, while clutching a small glass pickle jar with the other.

Now I must tell you that the court in Chelm was in session only when the occasion arose. The location varied, depending on what day of the week it was. Since it was Tuesday, the courtroom was at Herschel the Banker's office, which explains why Herschel the Banker was the presiding judge. But word of the case had spread, and Herschel's office was overflowing with curious onlookers.

"The court will come to order," announced Herschel, while banging his coffee mug on his desk like a gavel. "Jacob, present your case."

The baker told the court what had happened the day before and ended with this claim: "He filled his nose with the smell of my pastries then stood there drooling with an idiotic grin on his face."

"Izzy, what do you have to say for yourself?" the banker asked.

"I was hungry, Your Honor, and was so overcome by the aroma of the pastries that I just stood there and enjoyed the smell. I beg for mercy. I am just a poor tailor with a family to support."

Herschel then tapped on his coffee mug with his spoon. "It's an open and shut case. You filled your nose with the smell of Jacob the Baker's pastries. The court finds you guilty as charged and orders you to pay the fine of one zloty."

Jacob the Baker smiled broadly as friends congratulated him on his court victory. Merchants lined up to shake Herschel the Banker's hand and pat him on the back. "A wise decision," they said.

Izzy, dejected, stepped forward to pay the fine. But Sarah grabbed his hand, pulling him back. "Excuse me, Your Honor. I have come to pay my father's fine with money I've saved in this pickle jar." She held up a glass jar full of coins. The room was suddenly quiet as all eyes turned to the girl.

Then Sarah shook the pickle jar. The sound of coins jingling filled the room. "Your Honor, I wonder if the baker can hear the zlotys jingling in my pickle jar?"

"Of course I can hear them," Jacob the Baker snapped gruffly.

"Good. My father filled his nose with the smell of your pastries and now you have filled your ears with the sound of my money." Then, turning to the judge, she said, "Your Honor, the fine has been paid."

The courtroom buzzed as Herschel the Banker banged his coffee mug on the desk and announced, "Paid in full. Case closed!"

Izzy picked up Sarah and hugged her tightly. "This is the hug I forgot to give you when I came home last night."

On the Way to Broken Bow

AN ORIGINAL STORY BY MARIANNE J. DYSON

Airplane Jargon:
Roger: word used in radio communications that means "message received."

It wasn't the best day for flying in a small plane. The air was bouncy, and scattered storm clouds made an obstacle course of the route between Fort Worth, Texas, and Broken Bow, Oklahoma. Kimberly didn't mind. She loved to fly with her mom; in an airplane, her wheelchair didn't hold her back. But their eleven-year-old passenger, Cohita, was scared. The girl's eyes looked enormous amid all the white bandages protecting her burned skin.

Kimberly's mom flew with Angel Flight, a group of volunteer pilots who carried patients to and from hospitals around the country free of charge. Cohita had just been released from a burn center in Texas, and Kimberly's mom was flying her home to Broken Bow. Kimberly's job was to help Cohita feel at ease during her first flight in a small plane.

But the weather was making Kimberly's job difficult today. At every flash of distant lightning, Cohita yelped, reminded of the flash fire that had burned her face and scalp. Kimberly needed to get her thinking about something else.

"Hey, Cohita," Kimberly called. Cohita looked up from the stuffed bear the social workers had given her. Kimberly held up an aviation map. "See these blue tepees?" Cohita nodded. "These are symbols for towers. The tallest one is 987 feet. If we can find it, we'll know exactly where we are. Want to help?"

"I guess so," Cohita said.

Kimberly smiled. "Great! It should have blinking red lights on top."

Almost immediately Cohita asked, "Is that it over there?"

Kimberly looked where Cohita pointed. She couldn't spot the tower, so she lifted a pair of binoculars to her eyes. There it was blinking steadily in the distance. "Wow, you must have the eyes of an eagle!" she said.

"Yes, but it doesn't matter," Cohita mumbled.

Kimberly frowned. "Why do you say that?"

"Because I'm a monster!" Cohita wailed. "I will never have any friends." She sighed and hung her head.

Kimberly's mother glanced over. Kimberly nodded and said, "I thought that, too, right after my accident."

Cohita's head jerked up. Kimberly plunged into her story. "It happened at summer camp. I was nine. Some girls I thought were my friends dared me to pet Black Lightning, a wild stallion. They were mad at me, I guess, and wanted to get me in trouble for being in the stallion's pen." Even after four years, the memory stung. "He reared up and landed right on top of me. I'll never forget the sound of that moment: laughter, Black Lightning's terrified neighing, and the snap of my spine."

"That's horrible!" Cohita said.

Kimberly nodded. "Some friends, huh? And the girls who told you to wash your hair with gasoline . . . It's better to have no friends than friends like that."

Cohita stared down at her bear. "I was stupid to listen to them. They said it would make my hair thick and shiny." Cohita blotted her eyes with a tissue. "Now I have no hair at all!"

Kimberly knew that helpless feeling all too well. "There's nothing you can do about that," she said gently. "You have to focus on things you can do." The plane jostled a bit in the turbulent air. "Like using those eagle eyes to help me find where we are on the map."

Kimberly's mom smiled. "Speaking of maps, will you hold the yoke for me while I search under the seat for the next one?"

"Sure!" Kimberly said.

"What's a yoke?" Cohita asked.

"A yoke is a steering wheel," Kimberly said. "There are two and they work together. That way either the pilot or the copilot can fly the plane." Kimberly turned her yoke to the right, and her mother's yoke turned right, too. "See?"

"Like two friends, always dancing together—" Cohita stopped herself and looked apologetically at Kimberly, who would never dance. "I'm sorry!" Cohita said. "I didn't mean…"

"It's okay," Kimberly said. "I'd rather fly than dance anyway!"

While they were talking, Kimberly's mother undid her shoulder harness and dug a map out from under her seat. "Broken Bow, Oklahoma, is right here," she said, handing the map to Cohita. "We should get there in thirty minutes."

"Thank you again, Mrs. Gonzales," Cohita said, taking the map. "My parents couldn't afford an air ambulance, and the doctors said I might pick up germs on a long bus trip. If it weren't for Angel Flight, I don't know how I'd get home."

"I was glad to volunteer," Kimberly's mom said. She was reaching for her shoulder harness when a warning light caught her eye. "Oh darn!" she said. "The alternator is out."

"What does that mean?" Kimberly asked.

"It means the engine isn't charging the battery anymore. When the battery runs out, the lights and radios will quit. But don't worry; we're almost there, and I don't need the lights and radios to land anyway." She was reaching for her shoulder harness again when—wham!—the plane dropped like a broken elevator. The yoke jerked from Kimberly's hands, then she blacked out.

Kimberly awoke to Cohita screaming. The plane was bouncing like a bucking bronco. "Wh-at hap-pen-ed?" Kimberly stuttered in the shaking plane. Then she saw her mother slumped sideways with a nasty gash on the top of her head.

"Mom! Wake up!" Kimberly shouted, tugging on her mother's arm. With her shoulder harness off, she must have slammed into the ceiling! Kimberly's stomach rose in her throat.

"Do something!" Cohita shouted.

Kimberly grabbed the yoke and pulled back with all her strength. "We must have hit a wind shear," she said. A wind shear was like a waterfall in the air, caused when one air mass ran into another. At least the plane had not slammed all the way to the ground. Kimberly pressed the talk button on the yoke and spoke into her headset's microphone. "Whoever's on the radio, this is Cessna 1-2-1-niner foxtrot. We have an emergency!"

"1-2-1-niner foxtrot, this is Forth Worth Radio. Please state nature of emergency and give altitude."

Kimberly looked at the altimeter. "We're at 2,300 feet." They had dropped over 2,000 feet already! "I think we hit a wind shear. My mom, the pilot, has been knocked out." Kimberly was not quite successful in keeping the squeak out of her voice.

"1-niner fox, we have you on radar. You are about 15 miles southwest of Idabel airport. Don't worry; we'll talk you in."

"Okay," Kimberly said. When she pressed the talk button, the glowing numbers on the radio blinked. The alternator! "Fort Worth, Mom said the alternator was out, and just now the radio lights blinked when I pushed the talk button. Can you hear me?"

"1-niner fox, roger, we can hear you. Stay calm; we'll have instructions for you in a minute."

Kimberly grabbed the yoke to stop a roll to the right. But she overcontrolled, and they banked left. Fists of water punched the plane, which had wandered into a thunderstorm. Lightning struck nearby. Cohita screamed.

"Stop that!" Kimberly yelled. "I'm scared enough without you screaming!"

Cohita went silent. The sounds of the droning engine and pelting rain filled the cockpit. "Mom, please wake up!" Kimberly cried.

With one hand on the yoke, Kimberly fished out the first-aid kit and pressed some gauze to her mom's head to stop the bleeding. She used her mom's headset to hold the gauze in place.

"1-niner fox, my name is Mitch. Who am I talking to?"

This was a new voice. Kimberly thought he sounded kind of like Grandpa. "This is Kimberly Gonzales," she said.

"Hi, Kimberly. Mind if I ask how old you are?"

"Thirteen."

"Great age, thirteen," he said. "I started flying when I was thirteen. 'Course, that was a long time ago."

"He's trying to calm me down," Kimberly thought. She realized just how nervous she was. Had she really yelled at Cohita?

"First, because of your alternator problem, I want you to keep your radio use to a minimum. The battery might last long enough to get you down, but every time you transmit, it drains it. Say 'yes' if you understand."

"Yes," Kimberly said. How would she get through this if she lost the radio?

"Good," Mitch said. "The next thing we need to do is bring you down to 2,000 feet. All you have to do is pull back a little on the throttle. If you understand, say 'yes' again."

Kimberly's voice bounced with the plane. "Y-ee-ss," she said. She yanked the throttle, and the engine grew quieter. Her stomach jumped into her throat.

"You're descending a bit faster than you need to," Mitch said.

A bit! Kimberly knew those flight controllers were masters of understatement. She must be falling like a brick. Kimberly pulled back on the yoke to raise the airplane's nose, then pushed the throttle in a little bit to give the engine more gas. Her stomach settled at about heart level.

"Great flying, Ace," Mitch said.

Kimberly had a feeling he'd have said that no matter what she did. But she had to admit, this guy knew how to make her feel better.

"Okay, pilot Kimberly, if the fuel mixture knob is not already pushed in all the way, push it in. It's the red knob right next to the throttle."

"I see it." Kimberly pushed the knob in. A gust of wind tossed the plane, and her mom fell forward against the yoke. The plane went into a nosedive!

"Kimberly, I recommend you pull back on the yoke to stop your descent," Mitch said.

"I'm trying!" The yoke wouldn't budge with her mom's weight against it. Just as Kimberly was about to remove her shoulder harness, Cohita reached forward and grabbed Mrs. Gonzales's left arm, pulling her off the yoke. Then she fastened Mrs. Gonzales's shoulder harness. "Cohita, you're out of your seat belt!" Kimberly shouted. "You could be knocked out!"

"So could you," Cohita yelled back. "Then who would fly the plane?"

Kimberly hadn't thought about that. She pulled back the yoke and swallowed nervously. "Thank you, Cohita. And," she added, "I'm sorry I yelled at you."

"It's okay. You were right. I was only thinking of how scared I was instead of how I could help."

"Thanks again," Kimberly said. She'd only lost a few hundred feet thanks to Cohita.

Mitch said, "Kimberly, do you see the airport?"

"No," Kimberly said. "But a red flag just came up on an instrument in front of me."

"It means it's not working. That's okay. You're real close to the airport. Descend to 1,500 feet. Understand?"

"Yes," Kimberly said. Her lower lip quivered in fear. If the instruments weren't working, how long would the radio last?

"You're doing great," Mitch said. "The airport is to your left. Look for a bright beacon flashing green then white. Tell me when you see it."

Kimberly didn't see anything but rain. A gust jerked the plane up then down, and lightning flashed nearby. At least Cohita didn't scream this time. But how could Kimberly land at an airport she couldn't find?

"Cohita, I need those eagle eyes of yours. The airport's to the left, but I can't see it. Try to spot a light that flashes green then white."

"Yes!" Cohita said, pointing to the front. "I can see the light through the propeller!"

Kimberly tilted the nose down and peered into the rain. She couldn't see anything, but she trusted Cohita. She turned the plane in the direction Cohita was pointing. "I see it!" Kimberly said. She flashed a smile back at Cohita.

"Good," Mitch said. "But listen: If the radio fails, just

keep descending to the runway. When you get over the big number 35 at the end of the runway, your altitude should be between 50 and 100 feet. Also, watch the air speed indicator. If you're going under 60 miles per hour, push the yoke forward or the throttle in a bit to pick up some speed. Got it?"

Kimberly gulped. "I think so." There was so much to remember!

"You're a bit too high. You need to—"

"Mitch?" Kimberly thumbed the talk switch. Nothing! The radio had gone dark. Need to what? If she were too high, she'd go past the runway. There were buildings there! Her altitude was 300 feet—wasn't it supposed to be 50 to 100? She needed to lose altitude fast.

Lightning lit up the wing. The flaps! They would help her descend fast without taking a nosedive. She pulled the lever. Whoa! Talk about dropping like a brick!

The ground seemed to rise at her. The plane hit hard and sped down the runway. What was that ahead? A deer! Unless she turned the plane, she was going to hit it! But the only way to steer on the ground was to use the rudder pedals. Kimberly's feet dangled uselessly. If she could only reach the pedals with her arms…The tow bar!

"Cohita—quick! I need the tow bar. It's on the floor by your feet!"

"I see it!" Cohita said. She handed the metal bar to Kimberly.

Kimberly jammed the bar against the rudder pedal. The plane skidded to the left, avoiding the deer. However, there wasn't time to change directions, and the plane sped off the runway into a grassy ditch. The landing gear smashed into some runway lights, jerking the plane to a violent stop with the left wing striking the ground. The cockpit was undamaged, and they were all alive. But fuel spurted out of the wing and burst into flames. Kimberly shut off the engine. It was eerily quiet.

Fire crackled and popped outside her mother's door. Luckily, there was a door on Kimberly's side, too. Her heart pounded. She couldn't move her mother; she couldn't even lift herself. She needed to follow her own advice and focus on what she could do.

Kimberly undid her seat belt and popped the door. Rain whipped in and soaked her.

"Cohita, I need you to climb over the seat. Cohita?" She didn't answer. Kimberly turned to see her staring wide-eyed at the flames. Kimberly reached back and yanked the bear from her grip to get her attention. "Cohita, snap out of it! You're okay. Undo your seat belt and climb out!"

Cohita blinked, then began fumbling with her seat

belt. In a few minutes, she had climbed out and dragged Kimberly away from the plane. Kimberly handed the bear back to her.

"What about your mother?" Cohita asked.

"She's too heavy for us," Kimberly said. "But now that we're out of the way, rescue workers can get to her more quickly."

She was right. In just a few minutes, a fire truck showed up. Two firefighters jumped off and ran to rescue her mother. They soon pulled her clear and put out the fire.

"Thank you, Kimberly," Cohita said, her wet hand squeezing Kimberly's. An ambulance pulled up.

"For landing the plane?" Kimberly asked. She watched as they loaded her mother onto a stretcher. "You helped a lot. Besides, we didn't have much choice."

"Yes we did," Cohita said. "We could have just given up. You showed me that I can do things even if I am burned."

"You can," Kimberly agreed, pushing wet hair out of her eyes. "Including making new friends—real friends—when you get back to Broken Bow. You'll know they're real friends because when you're around them, you'll forget about your problems."

Lightning flashed. Cohita didn't scream. Instead, she smiled.

Temper, Temper

ADAPTED BY BRUCE LANSKY
FROM AN ITALIAN FOLKTALE

Italian Words:

Lira (pronounced "LEE-rah"): Italian money. One American
dollar is worth about 1,500 lira.

Basta (pronounced "BA-stah"): enough.

Papa Giovanni was tired. Very tired. A drought the
previous summer had destroyed most of his crops, leaving very little to eat, let alone sell. Yet somehow his family had kept food on the table through the cold winter.
Papa Giovanni and his eldest son, Marco, had worked
odd jobs in town. His wife, Marcella, had awakened at
five o'clock every morning to gather eggs and milk the
cows. His second son, Nico, had delivered fresh milk and
eggs to neighbors. His daughter, Francesca, had tutored
children. Everyone had pitched in.

Now it was spring. But the rolling hills of Tuscany were not covered with lush green grass and budding trees. They were brown. Looking at the parched earth and sniffing the dusty air, Papa Giovanni made a decision.

That evening as the family ate a meager dinner of plain pasta, Papa Giovanni gazed sadly at their tired faces and said, "We don't have enough money to buy seeds. And even if we did, we don't even have enough water to grow weeds. I'm sorry to say that this farm can no longer support our family." He turned to Marco. "Marco, you are my oldest son. I must ask you to leave home and make your own way in the world. When you get a job, please send some money home until we get some rain. Good luck."

"I'll do my best, Papa," Marco replied dutifully.

The next morning Marco hugged his family good-bye and started off down the road with a spring in his step and hope in his heart. He was big and strong. He knew that his hardworking parents had done all they could for him. Now it was his turn to help them.

He walked until he came to a green valley. A stream rushed beside fields green with sprouting corn and wheat. Marco noticed a large farmhouse. A sign at the gate read "Help Wanted."

"This farm seems to be prosperous," thought Marco.

"I'll try my luck here." He walked up the path to the front door and knocked.

It wasn't long before a beady-eyed farmer opened the door. "What do you want?" he asked.

"I'm looking for work," answered Marco. "Is the job still open?"

"Yes. Our field hand just quit. It isn't easy finding reliable help," the farmer replied grimly.

"You won't have to worry about me," said Marco. "I am as strong as an ox and won't quit until the job is done."

"You look strong enough," replied the farmer, "but you must prove you're not a quitter. If you leave before the crops are harvested, you won't get a single lira. If you stay, I'll give you ten million lira—more than most workers make in five years."

To Marco this job seemed almost too good to be true. If he stayed on the job until harvest, he would make enough money to buy his family a new farm. "It's a deal!" he said.

Marco worked hard all summer weeding, watering, and fertilizing the crops and caring for the livestock. His room was comfortable, and he was given plenty of food and drink each day. He didn't see much of the farmer, but didn't think much of it. The only thing on Marco's mind was all the money he would receive after the crops were harvested.

But when harvest time came, things changed. Marco was served bread and water at breakfast, instead of ham and eggs. When Marco sat down in the field to eat lunch, the farmer rode up on a horse, cracked his whip, and shouted, "Get back to work, you sluggard. I should have known better than to hire you."

Marco was confused. "What are you talking about? I've worked hard all morning in the hot sun. I just stopped for lunch."

The farmer cracked his whip again, knocking Marco's bread out of his hand. "There's no time for lunch. Get back to work."

Burning with silent anger, Marco brushed the bread-crumbs from his pants, wiped his brow, and went back to picking corn.

That night no pasta and wine sat on Marco's dinner table—just a slice of bread and a glass of water. At four o'clock the next morning, a loud knocking at the door awakened Marco.

"Why are you still sleeping when you should be out in the field picking corn? If I'd known you were so lazy, I never would have hired you."

Marco grumbled as he dressed in the dark. No bread

waited on the breakfast table—just a pitcher of water. He drank some and splashed the rest on his face to wake himself up. Then, tired and hungry, he walked slowly out to the fields.

Marco worked hard all morning. When the sun was directly overhead, he started walking back to the farm-house for lunch. Up rode the farmer on his horse, crack-ing his whip in the air. "Get back to work, you weakling!" shouted the farmer.

Marco held his temper. "Don't worry; I'll go back to work as soon as I've had some lunch."

But the farmer kept goading him. "What kind of ter-rible parents would raise a good-for-nothing like you?"

"That does it!" flashed Marco. "When you insult my family, you go too far. I've put up with a lot of abuse, but I won't stand for it any longer. I quit!"

The farmer started to laugh. "I knew you were a quit-ter the moment I laid eyes on you. Since you've quit before the crops are harvested, you won't get paid. Pick up your belongings and get off my property."

Marco trudged homeward with the farmer's cruel laughter ringing in his ears. He kept thinking about all the money he would have earned if he had finished har-vesting the crops. He had left home with hope in his heart, but now he had only tears in his eyes.

Papa Giovanni was looking out the window when Marco turned up the path. He noticed Marco's stooped shoulders and slow stride. He greeted his son with an embrace. Marco sobbed softly as he sank into his father's welcoming arms.

After supper the family crowded around Marco, and he told his sad story. Francesca was the first to comment. "You almost made it, Marco. Don't feel bad. That stingy crook took advantage of you. He worked you hard all summer, then tricked you into quitting."

"I'm proud of you," said Papa Giovanni. "You showed great restraint and only lost your temper when the farmer insulted your family. Now we know where ten million lira may be earned. Next year Nico can go back there and get it for us."

"I can't wait till spring, Papa," agreed Nico.

Papa Giovanni's family survived the winter as they had the previous year. By early spring, Nico was itching to get even with the cruel farmer.

As Nico set off down the road one morning, Marco yelled, "Remember, Nico, don't lose your temper—no matter what that buzzard says."

"Don't worry, Marco. I'll be back with the money this fall," Nico yelled back cheerfully.

Although Nico was not as big as his brother Marco,

he was a very hard worker. Walking briskly down the road, Nico arrived at the stingy farmer's door before dark.

The farmer told Nico he needed a reliable worker who would not quit before the crops were harvested. He offered Nico ten million lira if he would work all summer, but no pay if he quit.

"It's a deal," said Nico with a smile. He knew what to expect. He would hold his temper no matter what.

Summer went smoothly for Nico, as it had for Marco. He worked hard, ate well, and was left alone. But when harvest time drew near, the cruel farmer began to harass Nico.

On the first harvest day, he rapped on Nico's door at four in the morning. "There's no time for breakfast today. So get going, you worthless mutt."

Nico grumbled, but controlled his temper. He knew that the war of nerves had begun.

The farmer said, "Don't bother coming in for lunch. I'll bring you something to eat." But when the sun was directly overhead, the farmer did not show up.

In fact, he didn't show up until five in the afternoon. He carried a bucket of dirty water. "Here's your lunch, you louse."

Nico stared at the cruel farmer but didn't say a word.

He just kept working. The farmer went back to the farm-house.

The next morning Nico awoke with a cold shock. The farmer had dumped a bucket of icy water on him. "You forgot your lunch," he sneered. "Today I want you to get an early start. I won't have you dawdling like that lazy bum who worked here last summer."

Still half asleep, Nico spoke without thinking. "How dare you talk about my brother that way? He was the best worker you ever had, you miserable miser."

The farmer just sneered, "You take after your lazy brother and your stupid parents."

Lying in bed drenched with cold water, Nico lost his temper. "That does it! You are more cruel and stingy than I ever thought possible. I quit!"

Realizing what he had said, Nico came to his senses. "I'm sorry I said that, sir. I lost my temper. Please, let me keep my job."

But the cruel farmer was laughing so loudly, he didn't hear Nico's apology. "I knew you were a quitter from the moment I met you. Now get off my property. And don't expect any pay for your work."

Nico got dressed in the dark and left, grieving because the stingy farmer had outsmarted him just as he had outsmarted Marco. On the long walk home, he kept thinking of how close he had come to earning ten million lira for his needy family.

That night, his sister Francesca comforted him. "Don't torture yourself, Nico. You almost pulled it off. Now, if I can learn from your experience, I think we'll have that ten million lira in our hands by next fall."

Papa Giovanni couldn't believe his ears. "Forget it, Francesca. Your brothers worked hard for two summers and didn't make a single lira. That farmer is a smart crook. Try your luck elsewhere."

"But Papa, I won't make the same mistakes my brothers made. I'll figure out a new way to separate that crook from his cash." Francesca had made up her mind, and no one could change it.

All winter she thought about how to outwit the farmer. When the first buds of spring appeared on the trees, she said good-bye to her family and walked down the road to seek her fortune.

"Remember to keep your temper," yelled Nico.

"Don't worry about me, Nico," Francesca called out, "I can handle that old buzzard."

When she saw a "Help Wanted" sign in front of a prosperous-looking farmhouse, she knew she had come to the right place. She was all smiles as the farmer told her how hard it was to find reliable workers. She said,

"Don't worry about me; I won't quit. In fact, if I lose my temper, you don't have to pay me."

The stingy farmer could not believe his good fortune. Another goose had landed in his pond, and she was making it easy for him to pluck her feathers.

"Of course," continued Francesca, "if I stay until the crops are harvested, I'll expect a big reward."

"Agreed," said the farmer. "If you don't quit, I will pay you ten million lira."

"And if you lose your temper . . .," continued Francesca.

"I won't lose my temper," snapped the farmer.

"But if you should," Francesca persisted, "then the money would be mine. Do you agree?"

"Of course," said the farmer. He showed her to her room and said, "I want to see you bright and early tomorrow. There is lots of work to do."

Francesca smiled. "Whatever you say, boss."

At daybreak the next morning, Francesca knocked on the farmer's bedroom door. "You said you wanted to see me bright and early. Well, here I am. What would you like me to do?"

The farmer cursed under his breath. "Clean out the stables," he barked, "and when you're done, mow and water the lawn."

"Whatever you say, boss," Francesca sang out as the farmer pulled the covers over his head.

Soon he was awakened again by a terrible noise. He jumped out of bed, pulled on his clothes, and ran out into the yard.

All the horses and cows were on the lawn just outside the farmer's bedroom window.

"What's the meaning of this?" he demanded.

"I did just what you said, boss. I cleaned all the horses and cows out of the stables. They are now mowing and watering the lawn."

"That's not what I meant, you nincompoop!" he sputtered.

"Temper, temper," warned Francesca.

Remembering their agreement, the stingy farmer barked, "Go to the chicken coop and collect the eggs. Then feed the pigs."

"Whatever you say, boss," Francesca sang out as she picked up a basket and headed for the chicken coop.

Later the farmer dropped by the chicken coop and the pigpen to see how Francesca was doing. But he couldn't find her.

Then he heard a ruckus in the farmhouse. He couldn't believe his eyes when he looked into the dining room. Francesca had put plates on the floor for the pigs and was serving them savory omelets.

"What are you doing?" blustered the farmer.

"I'm doing exactly what you told me, boss. I gathered the eggs and now I'm feeding the pigs."

"You're crazy!" he shrieked.

"You'd better watch your fiery temper," she warned. "One day it will get you in trouble." Smiling, she continued to feed the pigs. The angry farmer stomped out of the dining room, afraid that he would lose all control.

Francesca soon followed him. "The pigs have finished their meal, boss. Now what do you want me to do?" she asked.

"Get those confounded pigs out of the dining room and sell them before I lose my temper," barked the angry farmer, trying to get rid of the nettlesome girl for a while.

"Whatever you say, boss," Francesca sang out as she headed for the dining room.

The farm was an hour from town by foot, so the farmer was surprised to see Francesca back in fifteen minutes without the pigs.

"Have you sold the pigs already?" he inquired.

"You told me to sell the pigs before you lost your temper. I figured you were going to lose your temper any minute, so I sold them as fast as I could," she explained.

"And what did get for them?"

"Well, on the road I met a man who asked me where I was going with the pigs. When I said I was taking them to market, he offered to buy them. 'How much will you pay?' I asked.

"'I have something worth far more than money,' he said.

"'What?' I asked.

"'Magic beans,' he answered. 'You may have heard of me. My name is Jack.'

"Well, of course I'd heard of Jack and his magic beans. You've heard of Jack, haven't you?"

"Enough of this nonsense," said the farmer. "How much money did he pay you for the pigs?"

"Money? He gave me five magic beans, which are worth a lot more than money. See? Here they are. Now I'll just plant them in your garden, and soon they'll grow as high as the sky."

"Magic beans! You sold my pigs for five beans?"

"Not only beans. Do you think I'm a fool? Your pigs are worth more than that."

The farmer, whose face had turned red with anger, breathed a sigh of relief. "How much did he pay you?"

"Well, he didn't exactly pay me any money. You see, in addition to the five beans, Jack also sang a song—"

"Wait a minute!" exploded the farmer. "Are you telling

me that you sold my pigs to this fellow Jack for five magic beans and a song?"

"Yes, but it's not just any song. It's a special song about pigs. Here's how it goes:

This little piggy went to market.
This little piggy stayed home.
This little piggy had roast beef.
This little piggy had none.
And this little piggy—"

Francesca never did finish her song. The angry farmer screamed, "*Basta! Basta! Basta!* Enough already. You're driving me crazy. I want you to leave this farm and never come back again."

"I'm going to miss you and your fiery temper," Francesca said sweetly. "However, the ten million lira you promised me will ease my sorrow."

The farmer ran into his house and soon returned with the money. "Take the money, but leave at once!" he said bitterly.

"Thank you," she said politely. "In just a few days I have earned the money it took you years to accumulate by cheating my brothers and who knows how many others. When people hear about this, you won't be able to find any more free labor. You'll soon find out what it's like to do an honest day's work—and I don't think you'll like it. I think you are a quitter. And when you decide to quit farming, get in touch with me. Now I've got the money to buy this farm, and a hardworking family to make it prosper."

Francesca returned home with a smile on her face and joy in her heart. Her entire family met her at the gate, and they all burst into cheers when they saw how much money she had in her purse.

"Now we can start over!" shouted Marco and Nico.

"We can buy a new farm where the corn grows as high as a horse's ears; a farm with a deep well and plenty of water," said Papa Giovanni.

"I know of a beautiful farm that just might be for sale," said Francesca.

Tulia!

AN ORIGINAL STORY BY JOAN HARRIES

Swahili Words:
Tulia (pronounced "too-LEE-ah"): calm down.
Nzuri (pronounced "n'ZOO-ree"): good.

"Aisha, I've asked you twice already: do you want ice cream? All you do is stand there holding that glass."

"Sorry. I was thinking about something else." Aisha put the glass in the dishwasher. "Ellen, do you smell smoke?"

"Aisha, every time you go with me to baby-sit, you imagine things," Ellen said. "When I sat for the Cohens, you heard burglars. Now you smell smoke."

"I guess I do overreact. Mom says so, too."

Ellen shoved a dish of ice cream into Aisha's hand. "My favorite," said Ellen. "Ben and Jerry's Cherry Garcia. Mrs. Brownell always gets some for me when I baby-sit." Aisha and Ellen sat at the kitchen table.

"Jake liked when you helped tuck him in," said Ellen.

"Did you make up that story you told him?"

Aisha nodded. "When you asked Mrs. Brownell if it was okay to bring me along, did you tell her I'm African American and…"

"No. Why should I?"

"Just wondered. Lots of people in Vermont act surprised when they meet me. I guess there aren't many African Americans here, 'specially—Ellen! I'm not imagining this time. Something's burning!"

"So why didn't the detectors go off?"

Aisha's spoon clattered in her dish as she jumped up. "My nose works better than a smoke detector. And it doesn't need batteries…which people forget to replace sometimes." She walked over to the stove. "Maybe Mrs. Brownell forgot to turn the oven off, and some spills are burning."

"Maybe. She's always in a hurry," said Ellen.

Aisha opened the oven door. "No, it's cold."

"Nothing burning in the microwave or toaster either. I'd better check on Jake." Ellen dashed out.

Smoke stung Aisha's eyes as she followed Ellen through the living room.

"The lights went out!" Ellen's voice shook. "Aisha, I'm scared."

"Who isn't?" Aisha grabbed Ellen's arm. "Jake! Come on!"

"*Tulia*," Aisha told herself. Aisha's mom often said that to her. Tulia is a Swahili word. It means calm down. Aisha's mother learned it when she studied African languages. "Tulia," Aisha kept reminding herself as she headed for the stairs.

"Don't go up!" cried Ellen. "Remember when the firefighter came to our school? She said, 'Leave the building immediately, then call the fire department.'"

"And leave a…" Aisha was going to say, "And leave a two-year-old to burn to death?" But there was no sense in talking now.

She ran up two steps. On the third, a blast of smoke overcame her. She slumped against the wall, gasping for breath.

"Come with me!" yelled Ellen. "I'm going out to call 911."

Smoke enveloped Aisha. What if she died of smoke inhalation? When Mrs. Brownell came home, she'd find Aisha's body on the steps and little Jake…

"Tulia!" Aisha told herself. She remembered the firefighter's words: "Crawl. The best air is near the floor."

Aisha sank facedown on the steps. Mouthfuls and nosefuls of dust weren't so great, but they sure were better than suffocating. Coughing and sneezing, Aisha dragged herself up two more steps.

The firefighter had said: "Cover your nose and mouth with a damp cloth."

A towel. The bathroom was at the top of the stairs.

Step eleven. Aisha heard sounds like logs crackling in a fireplace. She couldn't tell what part of the house was burning. What if Jake's room was on fire? She knew smoke could kill. And there was no sound from Jake!

"Don't get hysterical," Aisha warned herself. "Little kids can sleep through anything."

Step thirteen. She reached for the next step, but there was none. Just flat, lovely floor.

Aisha felt around. The bathroom door was open. She crawled in, felt the smooth, cool tub, and grabbed towels from the rack. She dumped them in the tub and turned the water on.

Wringing the heavy towels was a struggle. They were still dripping as she put one to her hot face. Aisha could almost hear the sizzle.

She draped another towel over her head and sucked in breaths of damp, filtered air. She held the third towel under her arm and crawled to Jake's room.

"Jake," Aisha called, forcing herself not to scream. If he panicked, she'd never be able to get him out.

After bumping into a table and who-knows-what-else, Aisha found the bed. "Jake." Kneeling, she leaned over him. She heard soft baby breaths. "Thank you, God," she whispered.

Bedsprings squeaked as Jake stirred and sat up. "I want my mommy!"

Aisha's instincts told her: grab him and run down the stairs. But dealing with Jomo, her little brother, had taught her she was no match for a kicking, punching two-year-old.

"I want my mommy," Jake whimpered.

Will he ever see her again? Will I ever see my mom? "Stop it," Aisha told herself.

"Jake, your mommy's coming soon. I'm Aisha. Remember? I told you the story about Lu, the lonely pig. And you kissed me good night."

"Aisha." Jake poked her towel. "Wet."

"I'm playing firefighter. That's why I'm wearing a wet towel. Firefighters cover their mouths and noses to keep smoke out. Do you want to play firefighter?"

Before Jake had a chance to say no, Aisha wrapped the towel around his head.

"I'm covering your face. You'll be a firefighter like me."

"Aisha and Jake firefighters."

"I'm going to pick you up and carry you outside. Put your arms around my neck and hold on tight."

Jake pushed her aside. "Pooh! Jake save Pooh."

"Dear God," thought Aisha. "Will we ever get out of here?" She grabbed Jake's arm.

"Ow!"

Tulia! "Sorry, Jake, I didn't mean to hurt you, but firefighters have to work fast."

By this time Jake had found Pooh. He took Aisha's hand. "Me go fast."

"I'll zip Pooh up inside your pajamas," Aisha told Jake, "so he'll be safe."

With Pooh inside his sleeper, Jake clutched Aisha's neck. Aisha held him with one arm and crawled toward the stairs.

Pain jabbed Aisha's neck as she sat down onto the top step. "Noise!" Jake yelled. His fingers dug into Aisha's neck.

"Yes, Jake, sirens. Fire trucks are coming. Jake, we're going to slide down step by step. You're doing great. Hang on."

They bumped down one more step. Ten to go.

On the fourth step, gravity took over. Aisha gasped as they tumbled down. Jake hollered. The towels fell from their heads.

They landed in a heap in the front hall. Aisha picked up Jake and stumbled out the front door. "Jake, we made it! Are you okay?"

"Jake okay," he whispered. Aisha figured he didn't have enough breath to speak louder. He'd inhaled a lot of smoke.

"Take deep breaths, Jake. Like this." As long as she lived, Aisha knew she'd never forget the taste, smell, and feel of those first gulps of fresh air.

Behind her, she heard vicious snapping and crackling. Her whole body ached, but she had to get Jake and herself away from the burning house.

Even when Aisha finally thought it was safe to put Jake down on the grass, she still held on to him.

She laid her head against Jake's. No need to say tulia anymore. Everything was *nzuri, nzuri, nzuri*—good, good, good.

Suddenly Aisha heard, "Hey, guys! It's the girl and the little kid."

"Firefighter!" murmured Jake.

Big, strong hands took him from Aisha.

"What's this in your pajamas, kiddo? Oh, I see. Here, hold Pooh. He's glad to be out."

"Jake save Pooh."

"You sure did, Jake," said the firefighter. "Now I'll take you to your mother. There she is, behind the fire emergency line. Will she ever be proud of you!"

Aisha heard Ellen call out, "Aisha, thank God you're all right!" Then she heard the firefighter say, "And you, young lady, are a hero! Follow me, okay?"

"Sir," said Aisha, "do you mind if I hold on to you?"

"You're going to pass out or something? Want one of the guys to carry you?"

"No, sir. I'm blind."

The firefighter was silent for a second. "Blind! Well, I'll be darned!"

Kim's Surprise Witness

ADAPTED BY BRUCE LANSKY
FROM A CHINESE FOLKTALE

Vietnamese Word:

Dong (pronounced "dong"): Vietnamese money. In Vietnam, people use dongs instead of dollars.

When Duc Tung, the moneylender, paid a visit, he always brought bad news with him. His scowling face and dark, formal clothes reminded people that if they failed to repay a loan that was due, the consequences would be serious. He would not hesitate to evict a family from their home if they missed a payment. His reputation for ruthlessness had spread throughout the Hanoi province in Vietnam.

Kim was pulling weeds from a rice paddy when Duc Tung arrived in a small carriage driven by two oxen. He stopped the carriage, climbed out, and cleared his throat to get her attention.

"I need to see your parents, young lady. Where are they?" he demanded in a brusque tone of voice.

Kim knew better than to give Duc Tung any information. Her parents would not want him following them around demanding money.

"My parents are very busy. You'll have to come back some other time," Kim explained politely.

"I must see them today," insisted Duc Tung, looking annoyed. "It is a matter of great importance. If you know where they are, I demand that you tell me."

Kim knew exactly where her parents were, but because she did not want Duc Tung to find them, she spoke in riddles: "Because you insist, I will tell you. My father has gone to cut living trees to plant dead trees. My mother has gone to sell the sun and buy the moon. And now that I have told you where they are, I bid you good day." Kim bowed slightly and returned to her gardening.

Duc Tung looked puzzled. He scratched his head and cleared his throat again. "Don't joke with me, young lady. This is a very serious matter. I will ask you one more time where your parents are. I expect a serious answer."

"My answer was not meant as a joke. You asked me

where my parents were. I answered truthfully. If you cannot solve the riddles, then I suppose you will have to come back some other time."

A sly smile came over Duc Tung's face. "Perhaps you do not want me to know where your parents are because you think that I have come to collect the money they owe me. You are a very loyal daughter. Your parents would be very proud of you. However, I have good news for your parents. I am sure your parents will be very happy to see me."

"I'm sure they would be happy to see you if they did not owe you any money," Kim answered shrewdly.

"How clever of you to guess," said Duc Tung. "Your parents will be happy to see me because I have come to tell your parents that I have canceled their debt. They do not owe me a single dong. Now please tell me where I can find them," he said.

"It is very kind of you to forgive my parents' debt," answered Kim. "It is also very unusual. I need a witness."

"But there's no one else here," said Duc Tung as he sat down on a log. Suddenly, he shrieked and jumped off the log.

"What's the matter?" asked Kim.

"I almost sat on top of a snapping turtle that was sitting on the log," he answered.

"It's only a small turtle," said Kim. "Why are you so afraid of it?"

"Well, if you must know," answered Duc Tung as he regained his composure, "a snapper bit off my little toe when I was a child. I've been scared of them ever since."

"In that case, this snapping turtle will be my witness," Kim announced.

"An excellent idea," said Duc Tung solemnly. "I swear on my ancestors' graves with this snapping turtle as a witness that I have forgiven your parents' debt."

"I believe you are telling the truth, so I will tell you where my parents are. My father is working on the riverbank cutting down bamboo trees to build a fence. My mother is at the market, selling paper fans that she makes to buy oil for her lamp. Thank you again for your generosity."

Later that day Kim's father returned home with his face knotted in anger.

"What's the matter, Father?" Kim asked.

"While I was working on the riverbank, building a fence, Duc Tung showed up demanding to be paid the money I owed him. I had to give him the bamboo stakes I had cut down. That man is like a snapping turtle. Once he has you in his jaws, he never lets go. I have no idea how he found me."

"Father, I am sorry to say that I told him where you were."

"How could you do that? You know how dangerous he is."

"All too well, Father. But he said he had good news for you—that he was forgiving your debt. I'm sorry to say that I believed him."

"You did your best. Now I must do my best to raise five hundred dongs. Tomorrow I must meet him in court with the rest of the money we owe him or we will lose the farm."

Just then Kim's mother came back from the market, looking upset. "That horrible moneylender, Duc Tung, tracked me down at the market. He took the money I had made selling the fans."

"He tricked me into telling him where you were, Mother. I'm terribly sorry," Kim explained, trying hard not to cry, for she felt that she had let her parents down.

"Don't worry, Kim," said Kim's mother in a comforting voice. "He would have found us eventually."

That evening Kim's parents visited friends and relatives, trying to scrape up the money they owed Duc Tung. And Kim spent the evening on the bank of the rice paddy, trying to remember everything that had happened that day, so she would be ready for her first visit to the court.

When the judge called the court to order the next morning, Kim and her parents were on one side of the room; Duc Tung was on the other, glaring at them.

In a loud voice, the judge asked: "Have you brought the five hundred dongs that you owe Duc Tung in repayment of the money he loaned to buy your farm?"

"Yes, Your Honor," Kim's father answered grimly, for he had gotten no sleep the night before.

"Bring it to me so that I can count it," commanded the judge.

To her parents' amazement, Kim stepped in front of her father. "Your Honor, there is no reason to pay Duc Tung a single dong. He canceled his debt to my parents."

"Is that true, Duc Tung?" asked the judge.

"Your Honor, the child is making this up."

The judge turned back to Kim. "When did he cancel the debt?"

"Yesterday, Your Honor, when he visited our farm. You see, he asked me where my parents were, but I would not tell him. Then he said that he wanted to see them so he could tell them the good news: that he had forgiven their debt. Naturally, I was so happy that I told him where they were. But when he tracked them down, he took all the money they had with them."

"Is that true?" the judge asked Duc Tung.

"It is nonsense, Your Honor. I didn't visit the farm yesterday. I had more important things to do," said Duc Tung scornfully.

"Well, young lady, I hope you have a witness," said the judge sternly. "I have known Duc Tung a long time, but I have never known him to cancel debts that are owed him."

"I knew no one would believe me," answered Kim, "so I made sure I had a witness, Your Honor."

For the first time that day, Kim's parents smiled. The judge's mouth fell open in amazement. "You do? Who is it?" he asked.

"I have brought my witness in this box," Kim stated confidently, holding the box out in front of her.

Duc Tung began to laugh. "Ha ha ha! The poor girl has lost her mind. She has brought her witness in a little wooden box. Excuse me, Your Honor. This is too funny."

Kim's parents squirmed in embarrassment. "Kim, don't be foolish," her father said. "Put away the box. Let me pay the money I owe and be done with it."

"If you have a witness in that box, I would like to see it," said the judge. "Produce your witness."

"I will give Duc Tung the honor of producing the witness," Kim said as she walked over to Duc Tung and handed the wooden box to him.

But Duc Tung refused to take the box. Suddenly, there was panic on his face and he yelled, "Your Honor, tell her to keep that snapping turtle away from me!"

"Ah ha!" exclaimed the judge, his eyebrows almost reaching the top of his forehead. Then, turning to Kim, the judge ordered, "Young lady, don't keep the court in suspense. Show me what is in your box this instant!"

All eyes were on Kim as she removed the top of the wooden box, reached inside, and pulled out the wriggling snapping turtle, which she held in front of Duc Tung. "Here is my witness."

Duc Tung leaped away. "That's close enough! That snapper almost bit me yesterday."

"It seems that you recognize her witness," said the judge. "It is obvious that you met Kim yesterday and swore that you had forgiven her parents' debt, with the turtle as a witness. I hereby order the five-hundred-dong debt forgiven. Furthermore, I order you to return the money you collected yesterday from Kim's parents," the judge concluded.

Kim let out a whoop of joy. But, as happy as Kim's parents were when they heard the verdict, they wisely refrained from hugging her until she had put her witness back in the wooden box.

For Love of Sunny

AN ORIGINAL STORY BY VIVIAN VANDE VELDE

Once upon a time, when dragons and trolls roamed the earth, the king of a small country on an island now known as Ireland invited the royalty from neighboring kingdoms to a ball at his palace.

Two of the people who met at that ball were Princess Meghan and Prince Sean, who was called Sunny because of his cheerful smile. Before the ball had ended, the two had fallen in love.

But when Sunny brought the princess home to meet his mother, things didn't go well.

"This is Princess Meghan," Sunny started. "Her parents are—"

"I passed through her parents' land last year," the queen said. "A nasty little kingdom whose most interesting inhabitants are the reindeer. Her parents keep pigs in their living room, you know."

Meghan forced herself to smile politely. She explained, "We let the pigs inside when it was cold so they wouldn't freeze to death." A bit peeved, she added, "They didn't stay in the living room, you know."

Sunny shrugged. "Anyway, we want to get married."

"Fine," his mother said. "As soon as she passes the tests."

"What tests?" the princess asked somewhat warily.

"You have to kill the giant troll that lives in the valley and the dragon that lives on the mountain. And then...let's see...you have to answer three questions."

"But that's not fair!" Meghan cried. "I have never heard of a princess having to win the hand of a prince."

"We have the rule," the queen purred, "to make sure our prince marries someone worthy of him."

"Wait a minute," Sunny said. "I don't remember hearing about this rule last year, when you wanted me to marry the royal chancellor's daughter."

"The rule applies only to foreign-born princesses." The queen smiled. "Good day."

Meghan waited until the queen left, then said, "What kind of questions, I wonder? I'm not good at riddles, and I'm even worse at history. I don't mind doing all the dangerous stuff, but I'd hate to do it only to fall on my face over who discovered what when."

"Don't be silly," Sunny said. "You can't go running all over the countryside killing dragons and trolls."

"We'll never see each other again if I don't," she reasoned. "Could you be happy with the chancellor's daughter?"

Sunny sighed. "She's nice enough, but I'll never love her as much as I love you."

"Well, then, I'm on my way," Meghan said, showing more confidence than she felt.

It was almost midnight when, halfway up the mountain, Meghan came face-to-face with the dragon.

"Hello!" she said. "How are you feeling?"

The dragon, who was used to knights sneaking up the back way, was a bit startled to find someone walking up the main road, even if that person was female, unarmored, and out of breath from the climb. "What?" he asked, scrambling to his feet.

"Oh, dear," she said. She spread her cloak on a rock and, from her pockets, took out a piece of parchment, a quill pen, and a bottle of ink. "Hard of hearing," she murmured while writing, tipping the paper to catch the moonlight. "I said," she repeated more loudly and distinctly, "How are you feeling?"

"No need to shout," the dragon answered. "I'm feeling all right. What's it to you?"

"Feeling all right," Meghan said, scribbling away. "No problems with your joints stiffening or anything?"

"No. Why?"

She didn't reply, being too busy writing down his answer. "I can't help noticing you're a bit overweight," she commented. "That doesn't affect your flying, does it?"

"Listen, little girl, you're treading on dangerous ground."

She started writing again. "Seems to have a touchy temperament," she read out loud.

"What are you doing?" the dragon screamed at her.

Meghan looked up, surprised. "I'm taking notes on your physical condition."

"But why?" asked the dragon.

"To know whom to bet on for the fight," she answered.

"Huh?" the dragon asked. "What fight?"

"With the giant troll," she replied.

"Now, why would I want to fight the troll?" the dragon wondered aloud.

"Because he's telling everyone you've been sitting here for too long—these are his words—on your fat behind, and he's going to come up here and take all your gold away from you."

The dragon hissed. "Let him try," he warned, smoke pouring out between clenched teeth.

Meghan pointed down the snowy mountain slope. The giant troll was pushing a huge empty wheelbarrow up the mountain path, stopping periodically to scratch his belly and yawn.

Earlier that evening, just as the sun had disappeared over the edge of the world, Meghan had awakened the troll from a peaceful sleep by sitting outside his cave and crying loudly.

"Shut up, or I'll come out and eat you!" he had shouted from his bed. Trolls sleep during the day and are awake at night, but this was much earlier in the night than this troll was used to waking up.

Encouraged, Meghan cried even louder.

"What is the matter with you?" he warned. "Don't you know that I eat people for dinner?"

"Oh, what difference does it make?" the girl wailed. "My brothers have killed each other fighting over the dragon's gold."

"Killed each other, eh?" The troll chuckled. "And what was the dragon doing during the fight?"

"He was just lying there dead."

"Dead?" The troll was suddenly very interested.

"Oh, woe is me! All that gold—more than enough for the two of them—and now they're dead."

"The gold!" the troll called. "Is it still there?" But Meghan didn't answer. She hid behind a tree and pretended she had run away. Then she watched as the troll stopped only long enough to eat a couple of sheep and to dig his wheelbarrow out from under a pile of unwashed laundry. When he looked ready to start up the mountain to loot the dragon's den, Meghan ran ahead of him.

Now, nothing could have surprised the troll more than seeing the supposedly dead dragon running full speed down the mountain straight at him.

"Hey!" the troll yelled. The dragon's claws reached out to crush his throat.

The troll picked up his wheelbarrow and brought it down on the dragon's head. The dragon turned around and used his spiked tail to knock over the troll.

On his way to the ground—and it was a long way for a giant troll—he pulled up a tree and jabbed the dragon in the stomach.

The dragon set the tree on fire with a blast of flame, but then got lost in the smoke. The troll took a running start toward where the smoke was thickest and bowled into the dragon.

Meghan watched the two of them tumble over the edge of a cliff.

"I'm ready for the questions now," Meghan said to the queen. The royal chancellor stood near the throne, while Sunny sat in his ceremonial chair, smiling confidently.

The queen signaled the chancellor to step forward. He still hoped his daughter would be the one to marry Sunny and had stayed up all night helping the queen think of impossible questions.

Sunny threw kisses across the room to Meghan, who winked at him. The chancellor cleared his throat, and the royal trumpeter played his official fanfare.

Suddenly Meghan screamed, making the same sound peasants use to call the pigs: "Su-u-u-e-e-e-e-ey! Pig! Pig! Pig! Pig! Pig!" Then she dropped down to her hands and knees and made grunting noises, all the while nipping at the chancellor's ankles.

The queen stood up with her mouth hanging open.

"What's the matter with you?" the chancellor cried.

Meghan jumped up. "Absolutely nothing," she answered. "Second question?"

"What?" he yelped.

"I said, 'Absolutely nothing.' Third question?"

"Wait a minute, those weren't the questions. You didn't really think those were the questions, did you?"

"Of course," Meghan snapped before the queen could say anything. "My! Those were three easy questions after all."

Sunny, who had blown a kiss after every answer, motioned the trumpeter to do another fanfare, then leaped to Meghan's side and kissed her. "My hero," he whispered.

The queen stamped her foot. "You horrible girl!" she screamed.

"You know, we have a rule in my country," Meghan said. "Anyone who is rude to the bride doesn't get an invitation to the wedding."

The queen threw her crown to the floor and wailed, "Oh, what's to become of us?"

"That's a fourth question, but I'll answer it anyway," Meghan said. "We'll probably all live happily ever after."

And she was right, for the queen calmed down and was invited to the wedding after all. The royal chancellor's daughter ran off with a juggler from the circus. And Sunny and Meghan ruled together for many peaceful years.

Emily and the Underground Railroad

AN ORIGINAL STORY BY JOANNE MITCHELL

Emily handed the baby to Mrs. Harriman.

"Thank you, Emily. I don't know how I would manage without you," Mrs. Harriman said. She leaned back against her pillow, cuddling her baby against her. "You've been such a good worker these past few weeks while I've been getting my strength back."

Emily smiled. Helping Mrs. Harriman after her baby had been born was actually easier than being home, helping Ma with the six younger children. The best part was that she was actually getting paid for her work. Ma had promised that some of that pay would go for new dresses for Emily. Now that she was thirteen, she had grown so much that her ankles were showing and her old dresses had no more hem to let out. The rest of her pay would have to help buy shoes for the other children. Emily knew that her family needed the money.

As she picked up a basket and started to leave the room, Emily said, "I'll be back soon to put little Thomas back in his cradle. I'm going to gather eggs now."

"Check carefully for that little speckled hen's nest," Mrs. Harriman said. "She always likes to hide her eggs. Once I found her eggs in the apple-drying shed, and once in the barn."

"I'll look for her," Emily promised.

Outside the house Emily paused for a moment to admire the small apple orchard that spread to the north of the main house. The trees were in full bloom now, brilliantly white in the bright spring sunshine. The rest of Mr. Harriman's prosperous farm grew wheat, corn, and oats. Here in 1853 in western New York State, these were all important crops.

In the chicken coop, sure enough, the little speckled hen was not in sight. She always appeared promptly enough when Emily fed the chickens, so she couldn't be that far away. Emily checked quickly through the barn, but could find no sign of the hen. She pushed open the door of the apple-drying shed, unused at this season of the year. In the fall, farm workers sliced and dried apples from the orchard in this shed; the drying preserved the apples from spoiling. The bottom of the shed's door was broken, and the hen could have entered through the opening.

"Are you hiding your eggs in here, you rascally little hen?" she asked, talking to herself. Suddenly she thought she heard something—was that a rustling noise coming from behind those crates? As her eyes adjusted to the dim light, Emily stepped forward to look there and gasped.

Her heart thudded hard in her chest. She was looking straight into the eyes of a woman who was crouched down, trying to hide. The woman held her hand over the mouth of a small child she clutched to her side. The woman and child were black.

Escaped slaves! Emily's mind screamed at her. Escaped slaves hiding right in the apple-drying shed. What should she do?

The woman's eyes held hers in silent pleading.

"Emily!" Mr. Harriman's voice called from right outside the shed, making Emily jump. "What are you doing in there?"

Emily made an instant decision about what she would do. She could never betray someone who needed her help the way these two people did. She called out, "I'm looking for the speckled hen's nest, Mr. Harriman. Mrs. Harriman said she had found it here once." Then she whispered to the slave, "Don't be afraid. I'll be back later."

The woman nodded. She looked less frightened.

Emily left the shed, carefully closing the door behind her. Mr. Harriman waited in front of the door. "I couldn't find the nest," she said. "Mrs. Harriman suggested the barn and the shed, but it wasn't there."

"Well, get along with your other work," Mr. Harriman said. "I don't pay you good money to lollygag around."

Emily returned to the house, mechanically going through her chores. She put little Thomas to bed and returned to the kitchen. As she sliced ham for frying, made cornbread, and baked an apple pie from last year's dried apples, Emily kept thinking about the slave and her little girl.

Emily knew that even though slavery had ended in most northern states such as New York, the Fugitive Slave Act had been passed three years ago, in 1850. The law said that slave hunters could come into the northern states to track down runaway slaves who had escaped from plantations in the South. The hunters could find the escaped slaves, handcuff them, and take them back to their owners. Emily also knew that anyone who returned a runaway slave received a big reward, while someone caught hiding or helping an escaped slave would be arrested and jailed. Just last month a male slave had been caught in nearby Rochester and taken in chains back to his owner in Tennessee. The man who had been hiding him was in jail.

To be free from capture, slaves had to go even farther north than New York; they had to go all the way to Canada. That meant crossing Lake Ontario by boat. Emily had heard whispers of a group called the Underground Railroad that helped escaped slaves reach Canada, but she knew no one who admitted to being part of it. How could anyone admit it, when openly belonging to that group could mean prison?

The Underground Railroad wasn't a real railroad, of course, as she'd first thought it was. It wasn't even underground. It was just a name for people who helped escaped slaves by passing them from one safe spot to another.

If only she could talk to Ma or Pa! But their house was seven miles away, too far to go to ask for advice. They had always said that slavery was unjust and wicked. She knew they would feel the way she did. What could she do to help the woman and her child?

After supper Mr. Harriman announced he was going to visit a neighbor. As his horse disappeared in the distance, Emily wrapped up a slice of ham, the leftover cornbread, some cheese, a slice of apple pie, and a small pitcher of milk. She crossed the yard to the shed, first looking carefully to make sure she was unseen.

"Hello?" Emily said softly into the darkness inside. "Are you still here? I've brought food."

A shadowy figure rose from the corner. "Bless you, child. We've not eaten for two days." The woman took the food eagerly, but made sure the youngster with her had eaten before she herself took a bite. "Oh, this is good."

Emily said, "My name is Emily. What's yours?"

"I'm Juno. And my daughter is Pandora. She's three. The master, he named us all from some old stories he knew."

Emily asked, "Where did you come from?"

"A plantation in Georgia. I had to leave. The master was going to sell my Pandora. I was a house slave, and he said he didn't want me wasting my time taking care of Pandora when I should be waiting on the mistress."

"Sell your baby away from you?" Emily was horrified. "Can he really do that?"

Juno laughed bitterly. "The master can do anything he wants. So I left; I had to. No one is taking my baby from me. My man ran away a year ago, after he was whipped. He always told me that if I got away I should follow the drinking gourd, and I did."

Emily was puzzled. "The drinking gourd?"

"You know, those stars that make the shape of a drinking gourd with a long handle. They show you the North Star, and you follow it to go north to freedom. To Canada." She said the last word slowly, like a prayer.

"Oh, I've always called it the Big Dipper. You came all the way from Georgia? On foot?" Emily had never been more than twenty-five miles from home. She had learned about Georgia in school. She couldn't imagine someone traveling all that distance on foot, carrying a small child with her.

"Part of the way we got to ride in a wagon, hidden under some burlap bags. Some people—they're called the Underground Railroad—help people like me. They pass us from one to another. I got through Pennsylvania that way. Last night I was supposed to get to another station, a safe house, but I lost my way in the dark. I ended up here on this farm as it was starting to get light. I thought we'd better hide before we were seen."

Emily was worried. "I don't know how to help you get away. I don't know where you could go to be safe. Lake Ontario is only five miles away, and Canada is on the other side, but I don't know who would take you across."

Juno said softly, "Emily, you've already helped us. I can't get you into trouble. We'll leave tonight and I'll try to find the right house by myself. It's supposed to be a house made of round stones. It has white shutters and a big oak tree in the front."

Emily wrinkled her forehead. A house made with round stones. That meant a cobblestone house, made from the fist-sized, round stones gathered from the lakeshore and laid in rows with mortar. "That might be Mr. Carpenter's house. That's the only one near here like that, white shutters and all. But he's supposed to be a mean old grouch. I can't believe that he would risk himself to help someone else."

"Tell me where it is and I'll try going there myself. I have no choice." Juno spoke with quiet dignity.

"No," Emily said. If Juno had the courage to come all this distance, then she, Emily, would find the courage to help. "I'll see Mr. Carpenter at church tomorrow. I'll find a way to ask him if he has a safe house. You stay here another day and I'll visit again tomorrow evening."

The next day Mr. Harriman took Emily and the hired hands to church in the wagon. Mrs. Harriman was still too weak to travel. On the way he lectured them all. "I heard last night that some escaped slaves might be in the area. A twenty-year-old woman and her young daughter. There is a reward out for their capture."

"I don't know about slavery," one of the men said.

"Don't seem right, owning another person."

"The Bible mentions slaves," Mr. Harriman answered. "That makes it all right. They are valuable property and their owner deserves to get them back. Besides, there's a federal law that says they have to be returned."

Emily made herself as inconspicuous as she could in the back of the wagon. She knew Juno would get no sympathy from Mr. Harriman.

After church service Emily spotted Mr. Carpenter checking his horse's harness. She sidled over to him, first making sure that Mr. Harriman was busy talking to someone else.

"Mr. Carpenter?" Emily said.

"Yes?" Mr. Carpenter said gruffly. He was old, with a short white beard and an unsmiling face. "Speak up, girl."

Emily's voice almost didn't work because her mouth was so dry. Her stomach rolled and for a moment she felt nauseated, because of the big risk she was taking. She considered leaving and letting Juno solve her own problems. After all, Emily hadn't asked to be involved. But no, she knew she could not abandon Juno, not after Juno had been so brave as to make it this far on her own. She could not let a young child be sold away from her mother.

"Mr. Carpenter," she said again, more firmly. "I am Emily Woodhall. I believe you know my parents, David and Elizabeth Woodhall. I would like to ask you a question. Supposing, just supposing, that someone knew where an escaped slave might be hiding. How would that person go about finding a safe place to take that slave?"

Mr. Carpenter looked at her in silence. Emily guessed that he was wondering if he could trust her, the same way she was wondering if she could trust him. Each of them would be able to have the other arrested and jailed.

"Well, now, Emily, you have an honest face. I know your parents and they are good people. Would this supposed slave that your supposed someone found be a woman with a child?"

"Yes, sir," she said.

"Good. I have been worried about them. Can you bring them to my house? Tonight?" At her nod he said, "I'll expect you. Back door." He walked away swiftly.

That night Emily waited until Mr. and Mrs. Harriman had been in bed for what seemed like a long time. She tiptoed down the stairs to the back door, holding her shoes in her hand and remembering to avoid the squeaky step. She quietly slipped out into the night with the bag of food she had prepared earlier.

"Juno?" she whispered into the shed. "Are you here?"

"Yes, Emily. I was about getting ready to leave this place. My Pandora is tired of keeping quiet and I was afraid we'd get caught."

While Juno and Pandora ate hungrily, Emily explained what had happened. They were going to have to walk about four miles to Mr. Carpenter's house. Fortunately, a half moon was out, which would give them some light. It would be too risky to take a lantern.

They stumbled along the road, which had deep ruts from wagon traffic. Emily slipped into the mud puddles that were all too common on the road. Her leather boots became soaked and muddy, but she knew that Juno's shoes were cracked and worn out. Juno was also carrying Pandora. If Juno could walk without complaining, then so could Emily.

If someone came along, they were prepared to jump into the roadside bushes and lie flat. They knew they would hear a horse from a long way off. Fortunately, no one was out traveling in the dark.

Finally they came to Mr. Carpenter's house. They circled around to the back. There was no sign that anyone was awake. Emily knocked timidly at the back door. It opened suddenly, showing Mr. Carpenter holding a candle.

"Come in, come in," he urged, ushering them down a hall and into the sitting room. "Here," he said, handing the candle to Emily. He dragged the settee to the side of the room and kicked the rug out of the way. There, previously hidden under the rug, was a metal ring set into the wooden floor. Mr. Carpenter pulled up on the ring and a trap door opened, revealing a ladder down to a small basement room.

"Down there," he pointed. "There's a mat where you can sleep, and extra candles and flint. I have a boat to Canada arranged for tomorrow. Quickly! We must have you safely hidden."

Juno took a step forward. She stopped and looked at Emily. "I'll never forget you, child. I'll pray for you forever."

Emily's eyes filled with tears. "Oh, Juno!" She threw her arms around Juno and Pandora and gave them both a big hug. "I'll remember you the rest of my life."

On the way back to the Harrimans' house, Emily was tired but jubilant. She had done it! Even though she had been afraid, she had done it.

Emily managed to slip back into the house without being heard. Morning came before she was ready to get out of bed. She got through her chores that day almost by sleepwalking. Were Juno and Pandora safe, she wondered. Had the boat come? Had they reached Canada? Would she ever know?

The next week after church, Mr. Carpenter winked at Emily. "That 'package' you gave me got delivered safely," he said quietly. "The best part is that she found her husband. Thanks to you, they are a family again."

"And thanks to you," Emily said. She knew better than to ask how many other fugitives had found shelter under Mr. Carpenter's sitting room floor. "If you need help again, call on me."

What had she said? Emily couldn't believe what had just come out of her mouth. After all the worry and fear, she had just volunteered to do it again. But as she thought about it, she knew it was true. Nothing in her life had ever felt as good as knowing that she had helped rescue two lives. And she would do it again and again if she had the chance.

"Good-bye, Juno," she whispered. "I'll never forget you."

Carla and the Greedy Merchant

ADAPTED BY ROBERT SCOTELLARO
FROM A FOLKTALE

In the Sicilian city of Palermo, Italy, there once lived a poor shoemaker and his young daughter, Carla. The shoemaker worked with great skill creating fine leather shoes and sandals, which he sold at a nearby market. Carla helped in the shop by polishing the finely crafted shoes until they shone.

One day the shoemaker loaded his wagon with goods and hitched up his only horse.

"Wish me luck, Carla," he said. "I am going to the market and hope to return before dark with my pockets filled with coins."

Carla wished her father a speedy return, kissed his cheek for luck, and saw him on his way.

The shoemaker took a route that brought him onto a street filled with stores. As he passed by a shoe store, a wealthy merchant called to him, "Hey! Wait, my good fellow!"

The shoemaker stopped as the merchant approached.

"I see you do fine work," said the merchant, picking up a pair of leather sandals and admiring them. "Very fine indeed!" Then he looked at the shoemaker with a sly grin. "How much for everything?"

The shoemaker thought for a moment about how much he would have charged for each pair in the market and named a fair price. "Twenty copper pieces for everything."

"It's a deal!" said the merchant firmly and handed the shoemaker the coins. Then the merchant climbed onto the wagon, seated himself next to the shoemaker, and told him to step down and be on his way.

"What's this?" protested the shoemaker.

"Come now, my dear fellow, let's not quibble. You did agree to sell me 'everything,' didn't you?"

"Well, yes…but…"

"I take you at your word. Everything includes your wagon and your horse. After all, a deal's a deal! If you wish to dispute my claim, we'll go before the judge. There's one just down the street!"

In shock, the shoemaker followed the merchant to the courthouse. When they were before the judge, the merchant explained what had been said, and the judge asked the shoemaker if he had indeed agreed to sell "everything."

"Well…yes…" said the shoemaker. "But…"

"Then a deal's a deal," the judge decreed. "And you must honor it."

Dejected—without his horse, his wagon, or his pride—the shoemaker walked back home, with the cruel merchant's laugh ringing in his ears.

When he got home, he explained everything to Carla just as it happened.

"What a greedy old buzzard!" said Carla, shaking her head. "But don't worry, Papa, I have an idea."

Early the next day, Carla selected six of the finest pairs of dancing slippers the shoemaker had ever crafted.

"Let me try my luck at selling these," Carla said. Her father, seeing the determination in his daughter's eyes, consented.

Carla loaded the beautiful shoes in a wheelbarrow and was on her way. She stopped to wipe her brow when she was in front of the wealthy merchant's shop, and in a flash the merchant came running out.

"*Signorina*," he purred, as he approached. "You look tired. Perhaps I can relieve you of your burden!"

"That would be very nice indeed," smiled Carla.

The merchant looked in the wheelbarrow and studied the dancing slippers. "How much for everything?" he grinned broadly, thinking he would make another good deal for himself.

"How much do you offer me?" replied Carla.

The merchant reached into his pocket then held out three copper pieces. "Times are tough, Signorina. This is all I can offer."

"Everything in your hand?" Carla asked.

"Yes, certainly."

"Then it's a deal!" said Carla firmly and held out her hand for payment.

The merchant grinned slyly and slid the coins into it.

"Oh, thank you," said Carla with her hand still extended. "And I see that you have three lovely rings. I will have them as well, thank you. They are very colorful!"

The merchant was taken aback. "What's this?" he bellowed.

"Come now, my dear man, let's not quibble," said Carla. "You did agree to pay me everything in your hand, didn't you?"

Now the merchant was fuming, for he was a man prone to displaying his wealth, and on that hand he had three very valuable rings that glittered in the sunlight: a diamond, a star sapphire, and a ruby. They were among his favorite possessions.

"I take you at your word. Everything in your hand includes your three rings. After all, a deal's a deal." Carla continued, "There is a judge just down the street. If you are not content with our deal, we will go before him." And so they did.

The judge listened patiently as Carla explained what had been said. The judge asked the merchant if he had indeed agreed to pay "everything in his hand."

"Well...yes...bu—, bu—, but...," the merchant stammered.

"Then a deal is a deal," the judge decreed. "And you must honor it."

Reluctantly, the merchant slipped the beautiful rings from his fingers and handed them to Carla.

Carla put two of them in her pocket and held out the ruby ring. "I am not a heartless person," she said. "I'll bet this ring means a great deal to you."

"Why yes, it does, Signorina," said the merchant sheepishly.

"Well then, I would be willing to trade it to you for my papa's horse and wagon, which you have recently acquired," said Carla with a broad smile. The merchant, realizing he had been tricked by his own brand of trickery, agreed.

And so Carla returned home to her proud, grateful father with their horse and wagon, three copper pieces, and the two precious rings as a bonus.

Even today the people of Palermo tell of how the clever Carla outsmarted the greedy merchant.

Vassilisa the Wise

Adapted by Joanne Mitchell from a Russian Folktale

Vassilisa looked out the window and sighed. Would the rain never stop? Her brother, Nickolai, had been gone for days. He went to visit Prince Aleksei at court to pledge his loyalty. Now that Nickolai had come of age, he would be the Prince's vassal, as their father had been before him. Vassilisa had been left at their country estate, with Grandmother, to supervise the peasants as they tended the crops.

Vassilisa imagined Nickolai at the center of a lively, amusing crowd. What a grand time he must be having! What exciting tales he would have to tell when he returned home!

At court Nickolai fretted at the delay. He still had not been able to pay his respects to the Prince, who was much too busy to spare time for an unimportant country lord. The lively, elegant crowd at court made no attempt to hide their scorn for Nickolai's country accent and clothes. Would he never be free to return to his estate?

One day an archery match was held. The crowd cheered as one soldier hit the center of the target and then sent another arrow so close to the first you could not have fit a thread between them.

"You won't see shooting that fine in your little village," an officer remarked to Nickolai. "You have to come to court for that."

"Oh, I don't know," Nickolai said, stung by the officer's tone. "In my village we have many fine archers. Even my sister, Vassilisa, could do better than that."

"Oh, ho!" cried the officer, laughing. "Do you hear that, Ivan? This countryman claims that his sister can outshoot you!"

"I tremble in fear," said Ivan. "When can we hold a match?" The crowd laughed and Nickolai flushed in irritation.

Later that day a horse race was held. At the end of the race the same officer cried out, "Does your village also excel in horsemanship, countryman?"

"Yes," Nickolai replied, growing angry. "We have many fine horses and many fine riders. Even my sister can outride anyone at court." Everyone laughed, and Nickolai gritted his teeth.

At the feast that night in the great hall, Nickolai sat alone. Course after course was brought in on golden platters: spicy haunch of venison, wild boar roasted with berries, pigeons baked with honey. Golden goblets of mead were placed on the table. For all he tasted of these delicacies, Nickolai might as well have been eating gruel and drinking water. Other diners looked at Nickolai, whispered to each other, and smiled.

When the minstrels began to play, one of the courtiers said loudly, "I wonder if his sister also sings and plays better than any at court."

"No, but I can," said Nickolai. "However, I did not bring my lyre with me to court."

A roar of laughter went up from the surrounding people. At the head table, Prince Aleksei turned to look. At his side the lovely Princess Svetlana, his niece, also turned to look. "What is it?" the Prince asked.

"Your highness," one of the courtiers replied, "this country oaf boasts about his village and his sister. She can outshoot your best archer and outride your best horseman, he claims. And now he claims he himself is a finer musician than any of your minstrels. Alas," the man said with a smirk, "he cannot prove the latter because he did not bring his lyre to court."

"Come here," Prince Aleksei commanded Nickolai. When Nickolai stood before him, he continued, "So it seems you have a remarkable sister. What else does she do? Is she beautiful and clever and wealthy as well? Does she spin hay into threads of gold?"

Nickolai fumed at the mockery in the Prince's voice. "My sister is not wealthy, my Prince. But she is indeed beautiful. She has braids of pale gold, thick as my wrist and long enough to sit on. She is more beautiful than any woman in court." The listening crowd gasped.

Princess Svetlana stiffened. Her dark eyes flashed in anger. "Must I listen to his insults?"

"And she is clever, my sister is," Nickolai continued wildly. "Even more clever than you are, Prince." A hush fell over the room and Nickolai knew he had said too much.

Prince Aleksei stood up. "Guards! To the dungeon with him. Send soldiers to fetch this paragon of sisters to court, so that we may see for ourselves how exceptional she is."

Nickolai's servant, Pyotr, saw his master being taken away by the guards. Slipping away, he rode through the forest by the light of the full moon to warn Vassilisa. At the end of the second day and night, he arrived at the estate and found her about to enter the house.

"Mistress, you must flee!" he gasped. "Master Nickolai is in the dungeon and soldiers are coming to take you to court."

"What? Tell me all," she said. When he finished, she patted his arm. "Well done, Pyotr. You traveled fast and far. Now go. You need to eat and rest. I must think of what to do."

She walked back and forth in the garden, talking to herself as she paced. "Oh, Nickolai, your pride was always your weakness. What can I do to rescue you? How can I persuade the Prince to let you go?"

After some time Vassilisa had a plan. She ran into the house, calling her maidservants, "Katya, Sasha, come quick! Katya, find the robes the Tartar noble left behind when he visited my father years ago. Sasha, you must cut off my braids. And bring the dye we made from the walnut husks. Hurry! I must be ready before the soldiers come."

Some hours later what appeared to be a wealthy Tartar rode to meet the Prince's soldiers. Vassilisa's close-cropped, brown-dyed hair fit snugly beneath a fur-trimmed cap. "Is this where a young woman named Vassilisa is staying?" one of the soldiers asked Vassilisa.

"It is, but you are too late, soldiers. Vassilisa has flown. However, I am on my way to your Prince's court and wish to travel with you."

"Look at the golden threads adorning his caftan," one of the soldiers told the others. "Look at that fine horse he rides. He must be an important person. The son of a nobleman, at least. We must treat him with respect."

"A Tartar!" Prince Aleksei exclaimed when the soldiers escorted Vassilisa to him. "I did not know the Golden Horde was near here." He thought with fear of the large tribe of nomadic horsemen from Asia that had conquered vast territories. Why was this Tartar at his court, he wondered. Would his princedom be the next to be conquered? "You are welcome, young lord," the Prince added, looking at Vassilisa, who appeared to be a young lad, slim and well-favored.

"Call me Vassili," said Vassilisa. "I have come on a visit of friendship between our peoples." The Prince doubted her words, thinking that this Tartar had come to spy on his court. The Golden Horde had probably sent a lone young man so that he, Prince Aleksei, would not be suspicious. He had best be very polite to the Tartar. "You speak our language exceedingly well, and your eyes are blue, not black, like most of your countrymen's. Is your mother one of our people?"

"Yes," said Vassilisa. "But my heart is with my father's

people." In truth, her heart was pounding so hard in her chest, she feared it might be heard.

"Come and eat and drink with us, young Vassili," said the Prince. "You must be weary from your travel."

"I accept your hospitality with thanks," said Vassilisa, and they entered the great hall.

"Uncle," whispered Princess Svetlana during the meal, tugging at the Prince's sleeve, "Uncle, that is not a man."

He shook her hand away. "Of course he is a man. He is a representative of the Golden Horde. Do not anger him."

Princess Svetlana persisted. "Uncle, that is a woman. See the graceful hands? See the soft cheeks? No beard will ever grow on those cheeks. Further, she does not look at me with admiration, the way all men do."

Prince Aleksei was afraid to anger the Tartar, but decided to test him. "Vassili, we have welcomed you to our court. Now it is time for amusement. Your people are noted for their archery. Would you care for a match against our champion, Ivan?"

"Gladly," said Vassilisa, thinking with relief of all the hours she had spent practicing archery with her brother and his friends instead of practicing her embroidery, as she should have been doing.

In the courtyard a target was set up. Vassilisa and

Ivan both hit the center. It was moved farther away by ten paces. Again, both hit the center. It was moved farther away by twenty paces. Again, both hit the center.

"Let us try a harder target," said Vassilisa. She pointed to a large oak tree at the edge of the courtyard. "Do you see the branch that juts out to the right? There is an acorn at the end. Let us aim at that."

"I can barely see it," said Ivan. "No man could hit that." When the Prince glared at him, he nodded and took careful aim. The arrow fell short by a hand's width.

Vassilisa raised her bow and in a single quick movement let loose the arrow. It sped true to the mark and clipped the acorn from the branch. The crowd gazed long in stunned silence before raising a cheer for the marksmanship of the Tartar.

"You see? No woman could have done that," Prince Aleksei whispered to his niece.

"She is a woman. I know she is," insisted the Princess. "That took only skill, not a man's strength."

"Then let us test the Tartar again," said Prince Aleksei.

The Prince advanced to stand before Vassilisa. "Well done," he said. "Fine shooting. Tell me, young lord, are your people truly as splendid horsemen as they are reputed to be? Would you care for a race?"

"Gladly," said Vassilisa, grateful for all the hours she

had spent riding with her brother and his friends instead of spinning wool, as she should have been doing. "What is the course?"

The Prince pointed to a tree far distant on the horizon. "Around that tree and back here."

"Oh, let it be more interesting," said Vassilisa. "Put up some obstacles to ride around."

"Agreed." The Prince directed soldiers to place posts to circle around and a fence to be jumped.

When the race began, the Prince's champion got a better start and was slightly ahead. However, because she was lighter, Vassilisa did not have to slow her horse to make the maneuvers as he did. She was four horse lengths ahead as she crossed the finish line. The crowd cheered loudly for the Tartar as she slid from her horse, flushed and laughing.

"Are you satisfied?" Prince Aleksei said to Princess Svetlana. "No woman can ride like that."

"Nevertheless, I am sure she is a woman," said the Princess. "Try one more test."

"All right. We will settle this for good. No woman can outthink me," said the Prince.

Prince Aleksei called Vassilisa to him. "Will you play chess with me, young Vassili? I have a fancy to see how your Tartar strategy will stand up to my good Russian skills."

"Gladly," said Vassilisa, "I have played since childhood and welcome a match."

"Then shall we play for high stakes? If you lose, your Golden Horde will stay far from my city. If you win, you may ask one favor of me and I will grant it." The Prince shuddered after he had made the offer, realizing that the Tartar could exact a high price for the favor, but he could not now draw back honorably.

"It is a bet," said Vassilisa.

The chess set was lovely. The board itself was inlaid with ivory brought from afar and the chess pieces were of gold and silver set with precious gemstones. They played on and on. First the Prince was ahead, but then Vassilisa captured his bishop. Then Vassilisa was ahead until the Prince took her knight. The day grew dim so that it was hard to tell the gold pieces from the silver. Just as the Prince signaled for torches to be brought for light, Vassilisa cried out, "Checkmate! I have won!"

Prince Aleksei stared at the board. "You have beaten me." His face was pale. "What is the favor you will ask of me?"

"I will think and let you know," said Vassilisa.

That night at the great feast, Vassilisa sat with downcast eyes. "Are you displeased?" asked the Prince.

Vassilisa shrugged, ignoring Princess Svetlana, who sat pouting in the next chair. "I would have music to cheer me. I have heard of the skill of your musicians— let them play."

Every minstrel played, every singer sang, and every dancer danced. Vassilisa sat unsmiling. "Is it not to your liking?" asked the Prince.

"The wind howling across the plains in winter is more musical to me. I have a lyre with me, which came from a faraway land. No one in the Golden Horde can play a lyre and I wish to hear it played."

The Prince looked at his minstrels. All shook their heads. One officer spoke hesitantly from his seat, "Great Prince, remember the country lout who made such boasts about his village? He claimed he could play a lyre, if only he had one here."

"Bring him here," ordered the Prince.

Soon Nickolai stood before them, pale and hollow-cheeked. He looked in puzzlement at the Tartar. "No," he thought, "I am only dreaming. It can't be."

"Let him eat and drink," said Vassilisa, "and then he will play for us."

Nickolai ate and drank eagerly, for prison fare was tasteless and sparse. Then he picked up the lyre and knew it was his own. He smiled at Vassilisa and began to play.

He sang praises of his land, songs of verdant spring and golden autumn. He sang of honest sweat in the fields and the joy of the harvest. He sang of new birth and the love of a parent for a child. He sang of love and beauty and glory. Prince Aleksei, at first rigid with resentment, was soon caught under the spell. Nickolai sang and played with such sweetness and charm that everyone in the great hall was silent in wonder.

When Nickolai finished singing and playing, Vassilisa said, "This is the favor I have won of you. I wish you to give this man's freedom into my keeping."

"He is not my slave," said the Prince. "I cannot give him to you."

Vassilisa walked from her table and stood beside Nickolai. "He boasted that he could play better than any minstrel at court and he proved that he could. He boasted that his sister could outshoot and outride anyone at court and she proved she could. Will you not then release him, for he spoke the truth?"

Prince Aleksei looked down at the two standing before him. Two pairs of identical blue eyes looked back at him. For a moment the Prince was poised between anger and mirth. He chose mirth. He laughed until tears rolled down his cheeks. "How you tricked me! I truly believed you were a man, a young lad."

"Then was I not right?" asked Nickolai. "Is she not clever and skillful and beautiful?"

"You were right," said the Prince. "This time, at least, she was more clever than I. She even outplayed me in chess."

"But she is not beautiful," said Princess Svetlana with a purr. She tossed her glossy black tresses. "He said his sister is more beautiful than any at court, and that is not true."

Vassilisa clutched her cropped hair, dull and mottled brown. "Walnut stain," she stammered. "I did not want to look so much like Nickolai."

The Prince said gently, "Perhaps we should wait a few years to judge beauty, so that your braids can grow again. But now what we have here is more rare than beauty. We have a woman who is willing to sacrifice her beauty, at least temporarily, for the sake of someone she loves."

"Hah!" said Princess Svetlana as she flounced from the room.

"And now," said the Prince, "let us resume the feast. And you, Nickolai, will sit at my right hand, and you, Vassilisa, sit at my left. You must tell me more of this remarkable village of yours."

Savannah's Piglets

ADAPTED BY SHERYL L. NELMS
FROM A FOLKTALE

Just after the Civil War, when the American frontier was still being settled, few people lived on the Kansas prairies. Savannah, her mother, Liza, and her father, Jackson, were some of the first black pioneers in that Indian country. They came west in a covered wagon and bought a farm along the Blue River from the Pawnee Indians.

Jackson was a hard-working farmer who loved his wife and daughter. He'd started out working the cotton fields of Georgia as a slave but was now a free man with his own farm, planting acres of field corn in the spring and trapping red fox and mink by the river in the winter.

Liza, also a former slave from Georgia, now enjoyed keeping house, raising chickens, and growing vegetables in the garden for her own family.

Savannah enjoyed helping her mother take care of the chickens. She liked flinging golden kernels of corn around the yard for them to find. And she liked searching for plump, warm eggs in their nests. But Savannah did not like the feathers. She hated pillowmaking time; that was a very sneezy job.

Savannah also helped her father with his hogs. She liked to watch the big black-and-white Poland China hogs crowd in to feed, squirming and pushing and squealing. The hogs always reminded Savannah of her cousins sitting down for Christmas dinner.

Liza, Jackson, and Savannah all worked hard. They sold their corn, hogs, furs, and chickens for good prices. They lived a good life along the Blue River, until one Wednesday morning when Liza woke up feeling nauseated.

Savannah hoped it was nothing serious—perhaps something Liza had eaten that didn't agree with her. But that's not what it turned out to be. Liza had cholera. Many of the pioneers passing through Kansas on the Oregon Trail had been dying from cholera, and now Liza had it, too.

She died on Monday morning in the stifling August heat.

Savannah helped her father bathe and dress her mother's body in her favorite blue velvet dress. Savannah fixed her mother's hair one last time and pinned it up. She helped her father lift her mother into a homemade cottonwood coffin, then helped carry it out onto the quiet Kansas plain.

Jackson prayed a long, solemn prayer and Savannah sobbed, "Amen." They buried Liza on the tree-shaded hill behind the house.

Savannah did the best she could to help her father by cooking and cleaning, washing and mending, and feeding the chickens. She also sold their eggs and chicks and helped tend the hogs.

But that winter, Jackson grew more and more sad. Savannah tried everything she could think of to make him happy, but nothing worked.

One day, about a year after Liza had died, Jackson went to town driving his two mules with a wagonload of corn. He came home later that evening with a skinny woman in a red buggy.

"Oh, my," thought Savannah as she glanced out of the front door. "What has happened to my pa? He was so sad. Now look at him. He's smiling. He looks so happy."

Savannah could not believe her father's words when he marched into the house and began to speak. "I have found someone, Savannah. Someone to love me again.

I've been so lonesome since your ma died. Now I have Billie!

"I met her this spring when I went to Marysville to buy seed corn. She came all the way from Kansas City to visit her sister. I've gotten in the habit of spending some time with her whenever I went to town. We enjoy each other's company and have decided to get married.

"I sold the corn, the wagon, the mules, the hogs, and the chickens. Now we can both go with Billie to live in Kansas City."

"I'm staying here," Savannah said without a pause. "Ma is buried here. The farm is here. This is where I belong."

"Okay, Savannah," her father replied reluctantly. "You may stay. After all you are almost a grown-up. You can live in town in the winter, with the Ottens. In the summer, Amos Otten will stop on his way to the sawmill to check on you."

"Thank you, Pa," Savannah said, "but I wish you would stay here, too."

"Savannah," her father said, "this may be my only chance for happiness. I may not have another chance at marriage, out here in the middle of Kansas. I wish you would come with us. I love you, Savannah, but I must go."

"Good-bye, Pa. I will miss you. I love you. If you need me, I will be here. Remember me."

And so they left, but only after Billie had rifled through all of Liza's belongings. She took a trunk full of Liza's dresses, including a beautiful red dress that Savannah loved, the utensils, and all the dinnerware.

Now Savannah's father was gone, her mother was dead, and her mother's keepsakes were looted. The wagon was sold, as were the mules, the chickens, and the hogs. "All gone," Savannah thought as she looked around the empty rooms of the house her father and mother had built. "Well, at least he didn't sell the farm," she thought, glancing out the window toward the river.

A farm. Paid for by her parents after years of hard work. The land where her mother now rested. The land her father had just abandoned.

Savannah decided to hike up the hill, to visit her mother's grave. As she made her way up the path, she noticed something black moving behind the empty chicken coop. Savannah stopped still, watching.

Slowly, carefully, a mud-covered snout peeked out from behind the corner of the coop. Then another. Then another. Savannah counted ten little pig noses wiggling at her.

"Pigs!" she exclaimed. "Ten baby pigs. Where did you

come from? Were you hiding down by the river? Is that where you got so muddy? My pa sold your mother and father. He sold all of your other brothers and sisters. You are orphans. Poor baby orphans." Savannah thought to herself, "We are all orphans."

Savannah glanced around the yard. What to do with the helpless piglets?

She decided the chicken coop would be best. It had worked for the chickens, and it ought to keep the pigs safe from coyotes and foxes.

"I will put you in here for now," she whispered, as she shooed them through the open door. "At least I'll know where you are."

Once she had the pigs in the chicken coop, she sat on a fence to think. "I am all these poor little piglets have," she thought. "I must feed them. But, what will I feed them? Pa sold the corn."

Then she remembered the ears of corn still in the field—bushels and bushels of corn. Her father had sold the corn he had already harvested, but the fields were still nearly full of ripe ears. She knew what to do. She would gather the ears of corn in her mother's old bushel baskets and carry them to the pigs. Savannah knew that corn was the best food for pigs. Her father had taught her that.

She gathered heavy baskets full of corn and trudged

up the hill. It was worth the effort; her little pigs ate greedily. As time went by, they grew bigger. Savannah built a fence around the chicken coop so the pigs could trot outdoors whenever they wanted to.

Meanwhile, Savannah started tending the garden. When her mother was alive, they had a huge garden. Savannah had helped plant and hoe rows of vegetables. It was hard work, but Savannah could do it.

This year her pa had planted the garden, but it had been neglected. To get the garden back into shape, Savannah had to water it well, weed it thoroughly, and pick the vegetables. It turned out to be a good garden.

Savannah knew how her mother stored the seeds from year to year, so she dried and stored some for her own spring garden.

In October, at harvest time, Savannah had bushels of vegetables. She stored enough for herself in the cellar, then packed sacks of extra turnips and potatoes and took them to town to sell. She took six of her fattest pigs to town to sell, too. They had grown so big that there wasn't room for all ten of them in the chicken coop during the winter.

With all the money she made, Savannah bought back her father's mules. Then she filled sacks with peas and beans from her garden, tied them onto the mules, and led them to town. Savannah sold her peas and beans and bought back her father's wagon.

In November, Savannah told Mr. Otten she had to stay at the farm to take care of her mules and pigs. Somebody had to feed them. She couldn't just let them starve. He agreed and said that he would check on her from time to time. He said it looked like she was doing a pretty good job of taking care of herself and the animals and that her father would be proud of her. That made Savannah feel good, but it also made her feel sad. She missed her father. She missed her mother, too.

As winter approached, Savannah realized that the garden would not keep her busy for much longer. So, she decided to see if she could find her father's traps. When Savannah got to the shed where her father had kept his furs, she saw the rusting traps hanging at the back of the shed. She decided to use them. They were just going to keep rusting if they hung there without someone scraping and oiling them.

Savannah set her trap line through the timber along the Blue River. She had helped her pa so many times, she knew how to set the traps and cover her scent. She was happy to have something to do through the long, cold winter. Savannah was glad her mother and father had shown her how to do so much. She could build a fire, cook potato soup, bake bread, skin a rabbit, and tan a hide.

Meanwhile, in Kansas City life was not so pleasant. Billie was not the person Jackson thought he had married. She was always complaining about something. She was not as kind and cheerful as she had been when they were courting. Billie did not have a mansion, as she had claimed. Instead, she lived in a peeling, gray boarding house. Jackson had to spend half of his money to buy a decent house for them. Then Billie managed to squander the other half on frilly dresses.

By spring, Jackson was pacing the floor at night, unable to sleep. What could he do? Nothing was ever good enough for Billie. Nothing was ever fine enough. He finally decided to leave, to go back to the farm in Kansas. After all, he was a farmer. Farming was all he knew. Even when he'd been a slave in Georgia, he'd been a farmer. He could not make a decent living in the big city. He told Billie that she could come with him if she wanted, but he was leaving.

Billie decided to ride back to the farm with Jackson. He guessed that Billie just didn't want to risk losing her fringed red buggy. He wondered if she valued that buggy more than she valued him.

Savannah was furrowing the soil and planting corn

when she noticed a brown dust cloud swirl down the hill. She stopped working and stood up. "It's too early for Mr. Otten," she thought. "Who could it be?"

When she finally recognized the person driving the buggy, she could hardly believe her eyes.

"Pa! Pa! Is that you? Oh, Pa, I have missed you so much," she hollered as she ran down the fence row.

"Whoa," her pa said, stopping the buggy beside the cornfield she was planting and stepping to the ground. "Savannah, I've missed you. How could I have left you? I was so foolish. I had everything I needed right here," he said, looking around at the fertile fields.

"What have you done with our farm, Savannah?" He stood there amazed. "It's beautiful! Your corn rows are so straight. Why, you're a better farmer than I am."

"Oh, no, Pa," Savannah said. "I was just trying to keep the orphan pigs fed. That was all. They needed food. I was only trying to keep us all fed."

"Well, I'm home now," he said. "I'm home to stay, if you'll let me. I'm a farmer. I belong on this land. I'm not a big-city person. I love you, Savannah. You are my daughter. Billie doesn't need me. I'm back if you'll have me for your pa again."

"Yes, Pa! Of course I'll have you!"

They both heard the crack of a whip as Billie jolted

away in the buggy, its fringe flapping in the wind.

Jackson bent to hug Savannah and then looked around at the straight rows of newly planted corn. "What a good job you did, my Savannah girl! A real good job! I am so proud of you. Proud to be your pa. You saved the farm. You are my real happiness. You gave me something to come home to.

"And I have brought something back for you, Savannah girl," her father added, stepping out the front door, and returning with a suitcase. "Go ahead, open it," he said.

"Oh, Pa," Savannah gasped, after she lifted the heavy lid. "Ma's beautiful red dress! You saved it for me! Oh, thank you so much!"

Savannah and her father continued to farm along the Blue River for many prosperous years. Savannah always remembered the happiness she felt when her father returned. She also kept her mother's red dress until it was time to give it to her own daughter years later.

Shannon Holmes's First Case

AN ORIGINAL STORY BY STEPHEN MOOSER

In all my thirteen years, I'd never seen the streets of London so full of fine carriages. Like me, all the Londoners were on their way to the Royal Stakes horse race at Ascot Park.

My uncle, the famous detective Sherlock Holmes, had invited me to share a carriage ride to the races. It was to be a very special occasion for my school, Essex Academy. The Academy had burned to the ground just months earlier. Our good friend Sir William Vickers had pledged to help rebuild it with proceeds from a victory today by his horse, Incredible Start.

I never tired of my uncle's tales about the many mysteries he'd solved. His ability to coax clues out of the flimsiest scraps of evidence was legendary. Someday I hoped to follow in his fabled footsteps.

As we stepped from the carriage at Ascot Park, I couldn't help noticing that my uncle was drawing thoughtfully on his pipe, his mind miles away. He had been distracted a lot lately. A robbery at one of London's largest banks had been perplexing him for weeks.

As we made our way through the crowd, my uncle tipped his tweed hat to a distinguished-looking man in a long coat, then smiled at half a dozen others. Uncle Sherlock might have been better known than the Lord Mayor himself. He usually attended events like this with his assistant, Dr. Watson, but today he had invited me. I told him I considered it a singular honor.

"The honor is all mine," he remarked, patting me on the shoulder. "Though I've not been blessed with children, I think of you as my own daughter."

We strolled through a tunnel beneath the grandstand and emerged onto a fenced lawn. Beyond the fence lay the track.

"There he is: Incredible Start," said Uncle Sherlock. "A magnificent horse, don't you think?"

I had to agree. Incredible Start was a stunning horse: black as coal and swift as the night train to Southhampton, folks said. Sir William Vickers was

standing alongside Incredible Start while his jockey carefully brushed the horse's shimmering mane.

"Sir William!" called Uncle Sherlock, waving his cap.
"Good luck!"

When Sir William saw my uncle, he signaled for us
to enter the paddock through a nearby gate.

"So glad you could come," said Sir William, reaching out for my uncle's hand, then mine. "We'll soon have
that academy of yours filled with scholars. Won't we,
Miss Shannon?"

I curtsied. "You are very generous," I said.

"I owe my success to my education," said Sir William.
"Rebuilding your school is the least I can do to repay
the favor."

"It doesn't take a detective to figure out who will win
today's contest," said Uncle Sherlock. He patted
Incredible Start on the shoulder. "It's elementary. Your
horse will do as he always does—win by ten lengths."

Sir William sighed. "I thought so myself before this
afternoon," he said, "but there's been a surprise. A horse
called Midnight Star was entered by a man you know
well: Henry Bonner."

"Bonner!" said Uncle Sherlock. "Why, that's the
scalawag I helped put in jail last year for flimflamming
the city's carriage operators."

"He's little better than a pirate," I said, recalling how he'd promised many of the drivers accident insurance, taken their deposits, then tried to skip town.

"He's free already?" asked Uncle Sherlock.

"Released on good behavior," said Sir William. He snorted. "Can you believe it? Now here he is with one of the finest thoroughbreds I've ever seen."

Midnight Star was not hard to spot. He matched Incredible Start in nearly every aspect, from his inky coloring to his muscled haunches. The only difference was a white mark on his forehead.

Mr. Bonner, a man with a drooping red mustache and a shiny black top hat, stood beside his horse. He was talking to his jockey.

"Solved the Baron's Bank case yet?" asked Sir William, changing the subject. "Imagine: Someone just walked into that vault, picked up a bag of money, and strolled out. Why didn't anyone see the thief?"

Uncle Sherlock shook his head. "It is most baffling. The thief must work for the bank, but who is it? Every employee has a solid alibi."

"Is the crime unsolvable then?" asked Sir William.

"On the contrary," said Uncle Sherlock. "A piece of the puzzle is missing, but it will turn up. It always does."

"Perhaps the thief was disguised as an employee," I

suggested quietly.

"An intriguing possibility," said Uncle Sherlock. He tipped his cap at me. "I like the way your mind works."

I beamed at my uncle's compliment. "Keep at it, Shannon," he continued, "and soon there will be a new S. Holmes making life miserable for the city's criminals."

"One Holmes is already too many," a gruff voice interrupted. I looked up and caught the bloodshot eyes of Henry Bonner, who was holding his horse by the bridle and glaring at my uncle.

"If you don't mind, we were talking to Sir William," said my uncle coolly.

Bonner sneered. "If you're smart, Sir William, you'll spare yourself some humiliation today. Midnight Star will leave your nag in the dust."

"I don't believe I've ever heard of Midnight Star," said Sir William. "Where has he raced?"

"Morocco, primarily," said Bonner. "I purchased him from a wealthy sheik." He nodded. "Believe me. He's the genuine article."

"I have no reason to doubt you," said Sir William, ever the gentleman. Midnight Star nuzzled my neck. I ran my hand gently across the mark on his forehead.

"Morocco," I whispered into his ear. "Such a long way from home!"

I smiled and stepped away just as the trumpeters announced the Royal Stakes with a blast of their horns.

"Neeeayyy!"

Incredible Start reared up on his hind legs, startled. I jumped back, barely avoiding his flailing hooves. As his shoes flashed by, I noted that they were well worn.

"Steady, steady," said Sir William's jockey, clasping the bridle tightly. "Sorry, sir. He's been jumpy all day."

"He has good reason to be nervous," said Bonner as he led Midnight Star toward the track. "This could very well be his last race."

I watched Midnight Star walk away, his polished shoes reflecting the sun. He seemed like such a nice horse. It was a shame he raced for such an awful man.

"Well," said my uncle, turning back to Sir William. "We won't keep you any longer. We're anxious to see Incredible Start cross the finish line for Essex Academy."

"He'll cross the line," said Sir William. "Let's just hope it's in first place. Bonner has a very special thorough-bred there. Don't count your money yet."

"We'll be cheering for you," said my uncle. Sir William nodded, then helped his jockey into the saddle and led Incredible Start away.

"There's something wrong with that horse," said Uncle Sherlock as we left the paddock. "Did you see the way he reared up?"

"I couldn't help but notice," I said, hiking up my dress as we climbed to a spot with a clear view of the track. I shaded my eyes with my hand and crinkled my nose. Something smelled! The odor reminded me of the Union Jack Laundry on Beckworthy Street.

I turned my attention to the upcoming race. While the huge crowd chatted excitedly, we watched the horses take their positions in the starting gate. The Royal Stakes was one full lap of the track, with the finish immediately in front of the grandstand.

Incredible Start took the inside post and Midnight Star the outside. Once locked into the gate the twelve horses shifted anxiously in their stalls as they waited for the doors to spring open and the race to begin.

"No one can catch Sir William's horse," said Uncle Sherlock. "He usually starts slow, but he's got the inside post and blinding speed."

I hoped my uncle was correct. Essex Academy depended on it. Suddenly a tiny flag flipped up atop the starting gate. BRRRRING! The stall doors flew open and the horses bolted onto the track.

"They're off!" yelled a red-faced man beside me. He pumped his fist in the air. "Go! Go! Go!"

Incredible Start burst from the gate like a scared

rabbit and led for the first few steps. Midnight Star came out of the gate last, but he quickly caught up, sliced across the track to the rail, and grabbed the lead. The noise from the crowd was deafening. All the spectators were screaming for their horses to catch Midnight Star. I'd only attended a few races in my life, but I knew enough to see that nobody, including Incredible Start, was going to catch Midnight Star.

"Sir William's horse is finished," said Uncle Sherlock. He shook his head. "Midnight Star looks more like Incredible Start than Incredible Start himself."

I shaded my eyes again to get a better look at the horses. Once again I smelled something that reminded me of a laundry. The smell, along with my uncle's words, made something click in my head.

"More like Incredible Start than Incredible Start himself," I shouted. My words were lost in the roar of the crowd as the horses rounded the far turn and came thundering down the homestretch.

"Blast it all!" screamed the red-faced man as Midnight Star crossed the finish line ten lengths ahead of the others. Incredible Start crossed the line thirty lengths back, accompanied by jeers from the crowd.

"Sometimes even a sure thing isn't sure," said my uncle. He squeezed my shoulder gently. "I'm sorry about your school."

"The race isn't over," I said. My uncle glanced at the track, then turned and studied me.

"But the race is over," he said. "Have you seen something I missed?"

"Perhaps it's nothing," I said. "But do you remember when Incredible Start reared up?"

"Of course."

"His shoes looked worn," I said, "as if he'd spent more time on the streets than on the track."

"Curious," said my uncle.

"Very curious," I said. "Do you know when Sir William bought Incredible Start?"

"Two years ago, I believe," said Sherlock.

"And the horse was already named Incredible Start, I presume," I said.

"We'll have to ask Sir William himself," said my uncle. "Here he comes now. Sir William!"

Sir William had gone out onto the track to console his jockey. He now was walking back with Incredible Start. Sir William looked up and forced a smile.

"Sorry, Shannon. He just didn't have it today. Tough luck, I guess."

"I'm not so certain," I said. "Tell me, who named your horse?"

Sir William stopped at the rail. "His previous owner, I believe. Why do you ask?"

"My uncle told me he usually starts slow," I said. "If he is slow to start, why is he named Incredible Start?"

"Where is this leading?" asked my uncle.

"I think his name comes not from the way he races, but the way he was born," I said. I turned back to Sir William. "In school I learned that identical twins are rare among horses."

"It's true," said Sir William.

My uncle chewed on his pipe. "An interesting line of inquiry," he said. "Shannon, I believe you are on to something here. I suggest we pay Mr. Bonner a visit."

In short order the three of us were standing in the winner's circle, just off the track, watching a half-dozen officials congratulate Henry Bonner. Just as a tall gentleman in a purple coat was handing him a silver trophy and the prize money, I cleared my throat loudly.

"You're awarding the trophy to the wrong man," I said. "The horse that won the race belongs to Sir William Vickers."

Everyone turned. The purple-coated man eyed me suspiciously. "Who are you?"

"A troublemaker, Mr. Haskins, that's who," said Bonner. His face turned as red as his bloodshot eyes.

"Remove her at once. This is no place for a child."

"If you will allow me a moment, I can explain," I said, stepping forward.

"Mr. Holmes!" said the official, Mr. Haskins, as he spotted my uncle. "Do you know this young lady?"

"Indeed, she's my niece," he said. "Please, I beg you: let her proceed."

"Very well," said Mr. Haskins. Bonner grumbled. I walked over and rubbed the mark on Midnight Star's forehead, then offered my hand to Mr. Haskins.

"Do you recognize the odor?" I asked, holding it up to his nose. Haskins thought for a moment, then replied, "Bleach?"

"Precisely," I said. "I first noticed the smell before the race. It reminded me of a laundry." I pointed a finger at Bonner. "I propose that he made that star by applying bleach to Incredible Start's forehead."

"Incredible Start?" said Mr. Haskins, raising a bushy eyebrow. "But the horse here is Midnight Star."

"He's Incredible Start with a bleached star on his forehead," I explained. "His exact twin was the horse Sir William raced."

"Do you mean to say that Midnight Star is really Incredible Start?" said Sir William. "This is terribly confusing."

Bonner sneered and shouted, "This is preposterous! How could I have found such a rare horse?"

"No doubt you discovered the twin while cheating the city carriage drivers last year," I said calmly. "The horse Sir William raced today has worn shoes. It is not a race horse—it's a workhorse used to pounding our cobbled streets."

"Outrageous!" thundered Mr. Bonner. He reached for the money in Mr. Haskins's hand, but the official quickly yanked it away. "Not so fast," he said. "First, I think we better take a good look at Sir William's horse."

"I won fair and square," Bonner grumbled.

"If so, then you have nothing to fear," said my uncle. "However, if my niece is correct, then you'll be facing charges for stealing Incredible Start."

Bonner looked around desperately. "I don't have to put up with this," he said. He took two steps and vaulted onto Incredible Start's back. "Gee-up!" he yelled.

For a moment everyone froze—everyone but me. I grabbed Bonner's leg as Incredible Start ran by. "Eeee-yow!" yelled Bonner, tumbling from the horse. Ker-flop! He landed on his back, sending up a cloud of dust. "Ooof!" he grunted.

"Incredible Start's original owners can confirm my suspicions," I said, dusting off my hands as Mr. Bonner moaned on the ground. "Incredible Start's name doesn't describe the way he races, but the way he started in life: as a twin."

"A twin?" said Sir William. "That makes perfect sense."

"Why, that's it!" exclaimed Uncle Sherlock. He put his hands on his cheeks and chomped on his pipe so hard I thought he might bite it in two.

"What is it, Holmes?" asked Sir William. My uncle shook his head in amazement.

"Shannon just solved the Baron's Bank case!"

"I did?" I said.

"Indeed, I think you did," said my uncle. "I'll wager that one of the bank's employees has an identical twin."

"Of course! It's entirely logical. One twin could have walked off with the money while the other was elsewhere in the bank establishing a perfect alibi," I said.

"The situation was so elementary, I couldn't see it staring me in the face," said my uncle. He clapped me on the back. "Shannon, you're a genius."

I beamed at my uncle. I couldn't believe it. I'd solved my first crime, and then my second, and all within a minute!

"Miss Holmes, you appear to have a great detective career ahead," said Mr. Haskins. He turned to Henry

Bonner. "And you, sir, are about to begin a career as a prisoner." Bonner just snarled at me.

My uncle took off his cap and placed it on my head. "You're a master sleuth, Shannon, if I've ever seen one."

Master sleuth! Though the cap was three sizes too big, I thought the title was a perfect fit.

Maya's Stone Soup

ADAPTED BY BRUCE LANSKY
FROM A EUROPEAN FOLKTALE

Spanish Words:

Burro (pronounced "BOO-ro"): a small donkey.

Adobe (pronounced "a-DO-beh"): constructed
of mud.

Tortillas (pronounced "tor-TEE-yas"): round pancake-like
bread made from corn.

Fiestas (pronounced "fee-YES-tas"): festivities.

Loca (pronounced "LO-ka"): crazy.

Deliciosa (pronounced "de-lee-SYO-sa"): delicious.

Gracias (pronounced "GRA-tsias"): thank you.

Por favor (pronounced "POR fa-VOR"): please.

Maya had spent a rain-soaked weekend with her
grandparents, who lived on a mountain farm in
Guatemala. It was summer, the rainy season. Maya had

gathered eggs from the hens. She had milked the cows. She had fed the pigs and watched them roll around in the mud. She had helped her grandmother care for a brand-new colt. But she was totally unprepared for what she would discover when she went back to her home on the coast of the Pacific Ocean.

On Sunday afternoon, Maya rode her burro down the winding mountain road, through the rain, toward home. As she got closer to her village, Maya saw that the road was covered with water. Straw and tile roofs had been blown off the houses. Debris was scattered everywhere. All along the way people were busy cleaning up and repairing their adobe houses. Maya guessed that a great hurricane had devastated the area while she was away.

As she rode on, Maya became more and more worried about what she'd find when she got back to her village. Were her parents and her little brother and sister safe? Was her house ruined? Maya was anxious to be home to help her family.

Suddenly her burro stumbled over something in the muddy road. Maya reined in the burro and climbed down to see whether it was hurt. After she made sure that the burro was all right, Maya took a stick and poked around in the mud to see what had tripped it.

After a short search, Maya found a big, round stone.

She rolled it into a puddle to clean it off. The stone was a beautiful reddish-brown color and it sparkled enchantingly. Maya wondered whether the stone might be valuable and decided to take it home to show her family.

Maya put the beautiful stone in her saddlebag, climbed back up on the burro, and continued to ride home through the mud and water. By the time she arrived, she wasn't surprised at what she saw. The hard-packed dirt floor of the house was completely covered with water. The shutters were gone, and the wind had blown rain in through the windows. Maya's parents were bone tired—they'd been up through the night bailing the water out of the house. Her little brother, Tomas, and her sister, Gabriela, were sitting in front of the house, crying.

"Maya, you're back! Thank goodness," exclaimed her mother. "Please take care of your brother and sister while we get the water out of the house. See if you can find them something to eat."

Maya looked for something to eat. The rain had poured through the kitchen window, soaking the tortillas in the cupboard. The chicken coop had been blown away; there were no eggs or chickens to cook. The garden was flooded. All the food was either gone or destroyed. Tomas and Gabriela were crying—cold and hungry. Maya had to do something. But what?

Hoping to borrow some food, Maya ran to the next-door neighbors. Their house was in worse shape than Maya's. When she asked for something to eat, they said, "Can't you see that we're busy fixing our house? Ask someone else!"

With the sound of her brother's and sister's crying ringing in her ears, Maya ran down the road to where a house used to be. It was gone. All that was left were some wooden planks, a bed, a table, and a chair sitting in a large puddle of water. A goat was nibbling on what used to be the vegetable garden. The neighbors were sitting on the bed, red-eyed and bewildered. They had lost almost everything. Maya didn't even bother to ask them for food. They needed help more than she did.

After trying a few more neighbors, Maya realized that everyone was too busy to care about her problems. She needed a new idea. When she got back home, she noticed her mother's big, black pot behind the house. It must have floated out the back door. Maya's mother used this huge pot when grandparents, uncles, aunts, and cousins all gathered for fiestas.

Maya picked up the pot and carried it toward the house. She thought she might cook something hot and nutritious for Tomas and Gabriela. But what? Slowly a plan began to take shape in her mind. "This could work..." she thought.

"Tomas! Gabriela! Come here. I need your help," Maya called.

Her brother and sister came running out of the house. They weren't crying anymore. They were glad to have a chance to help. "What can we do?" asked Tomas.

"I want you to look for anything dry enough to burn: paper, sticks, pieces of wood—anything," Maya told them. "We're going to make a fire."

"What for?" asked little Gabriela.

"So we can cook some soup in this pot."

Tomas and Gabriela smiled at the thought of finally getting some food.

"What kind of soup?" asked Tomas.

"Stone soup," Maya answered. "I found a very beautiful stone on the way from our grandparents' house. I'll put it in when the water is boiling. If you've never tasted stone soup before, you're in for a treat."

Tomas shrugged and pointed to his head with his finger. Then he twirled it around a few times. "Maya's gone *loca*," he cracked. Gabriela started giggling.

After finding a dry box of matches in the kitchen, a spoon, and a knife, Maya carried the pot to the small stone fireplace outside the house where her mother usually cooked. While waiting for Tomas and Gabriela to come back with paper and wood, Maya scouted for dry sticks and twigs and started a little fire.

But instead of helping Maya, Tomas and Gabriela ran off giggling to their parents. "*Mamá, Papá*, something's wrong with Maya. She's gone loca!"

Maya's parents looked up from their work. "What are you talking about?"

"We haven't had anything to eat in hours, so what is she cooking? Stone soup!"

Their parents shrugged and went back to work. They had too much work to worry about what Maya was cooking. Besides, Tomas and Gabriela weren't crying anymore.

When they realized their parents were too busy to pay attention to them, Tomas and Gabriela ran off to the neighbors' houses spreading the word: "Maya's gone loca! She's cooking stone soup!"

By the time Tomas and Gabriela returned, without any firewood, Maya had a good fire going and the pot was filled with water from the well.

But Tomas and Gabriela were not alone. A few neighbors had followed them back to see crazy Maya and her stone soup. Maya's parents interrupted their work to see what was going on.

"Tomas, Gabriela, hurry. I need more wood. You need

a hot fire to cook stone soup." The children scurried off to find some firewood.

"Are you really cooking stone soup?" asked a curious neighbor.

"Of course," Maya answered. "It's an old family recipe, and very *deliciosa*. When it's cooked, I'll give you a taste." Maya's parents looked at each other and shrugged, wondering what she was up to.

When Tomas and Gabriela had returned with armfuls of dry wood, Maya built up the fire. Then she held up her stone for everyone to see. "Here is the most important ingredient. See how beautiful it is?" Then she dropped it into the kettle. The stone splashed when it hit the water and clanked when it hit the bottom. Maya began to stir the soup.

After a few minutes, she dipped a spoon into the kettle and tasted the soup. "Not bad!" she said. "But it needs a little seasoning."

"I'll go and get some," said a curious neighbor. She ran home and returned in a few minutes with a small bag of salt and a peppermill.

Maya sprinkled salt and ground some pepper into the soup. Then she stirred the soup a few times, dipped her spoon into the soup, and tasted it. "That's a little better! But I think it could use a few carrots."

"I'll see if I can find a few in our garden," said another neighbor.

When he returned with some carrots, Maya cut off the greens, washed the carrots, and threw them into the pot. Then she stirred the soup for a few minutes and took a taste. "Mmmm! It's coming along nicely. But I think it could use some potatoes."

"I'll see if I can dig some up," said an old man who worked on a farm nearby. When he returned with some potatoes, Maya washed them, chopped them into small pieces, and tossed them into the pot. Then she stirred the soup and tasted it again. "Now it's starting to taste good," she said. "But still…it could use a little more flavor. Maybe an onion or two…"

"No problem," said the local innkeeper. "I can spare a few."

"…and a chicken," continued Maya.

"I'll catch one," called out a farmer whose chickens had survived the hurricane.

When the innkeeper returned with the onions and the farmer returned with the chicken, Maya cleaned the onions, plucked and washed the chicken, and tossed everything into the soup. Then she stirred the soup and let it simmer.

While everybody waited for the soup to cook, some

villagers arrived with guitars and began to play. The mood turned festive. People gathered around the pot and sang.

When she thought the soup was ready, Maya took a final taste. "Deliciosa!" she announced. "Now, anyone who brings a bowl and a spoon can have a taste of my stone soup."

The onlookers watched as Tomas and Gabriela ran to the kitchen. They returned with bowls and spoons, out of breath.

Gabriela was first. After her bowl was full, she took a taste. "Mmmm mmmm! Deliciosa. *Gracias*, Maya."

Tomas was impatient. He held out his bowl and clanked it with his spoon. "Can I have some stone soup, *por favor?*"

"Of course," Maya answered as she ladled out some soup into his bowl.

He slurped it down rapidly. "Gracias! May I have more, por favor?"

In a few minutes the crowd of villagers headed home to get bowls and spoons. When they returned, the hungry crowd had doubled or tripled. Almost everyone in the village had come for a bowl of stone soup—even the mayor.

When all the soup was gone, the mayor made a brief

speech: "I want to thank Maya for feeding us and cheering us up at a time when we all needed it." Everyone cheered Maya, who took a little bow.

"And I'd like to thank you," Maya told the gathered crowd. "My stone soup would not have been quite so delicious without your help. And if anyone here is ever hungry, I'll be happy to loan you my soup stone. I think you know the recipe."

The Peacemakers

AN ORIGINAL STORY BY LOIS GREIMAN

"We've come too far, Flint," Jessie said, putting a hand on her mare's dappled neck.

The doe they'd been racing was gone and the woods here were thick and silent. Mists curled up from the earth, seeming to reach for them with cool, ghostlike arms.

Darkness would set in soon and she was on MacDuff land. The thought sent a tingle of fear spurting up her spine.

"Father would kill me if he knew where we are," Jessie whispered. Flint tossed her head in agreement. "Take me home, girl," Jessie said, reining the mare away. But, suddenly, she heard a noise behind her.

Jessie turned and gasped. A horse stepped through the mist. He was large and black and upon his back was a girl about twelve years of age, no older than Jessie herself.

They stared at each other in surprise for a moment, but then the other girl spoke.

"Do you hate me?" she asked quietly.

"Hate you?" Jessie whispered. Who was this girl who had appeared out of nowhere? "How could I hate you? I don't even know you."

"But you're an Armstrong. I can tell by the plaid beneath your saddle." She pointed to Jessie's blue saddle blanket, then to the green cloth beneath her own. "And I am a MacDuff."

Jessie caught her breath. Her father had warned her about their enemies. They were thieves, and worse, not to be trusted—not like the Armstrongs who were honorable Scots. But when Jessie stared at the girl in front of her, she could see very little difference between them. The girl's light brown hair hung down her back in a long fat braid just as Jessie's did. Wisps of it had escaped as if she, too, had just had a wild ride through the heather.

"What's your name?" Jessie asked softly.

"Marnie," answered the other. "I rode out with the hunters, but I could not bear to see the deer slain, so I left them to ride on my own."

Jessie nodded. "I, too, hate to see deer die. In fact, I followed one here, for she was so beautiful to watch. But my father, the lord of the Armstrongs, will be angry if he learns how far I have come. He says my little brother, Douglas, and I will turn his hair gray, for we are always exploring in the forest outside the castle walls and pretending we are great heroes."

Marnie smiled. "We are not so different, you and I," she said. "For my father, the lord of the MacDuffs, would be quite upset if he knew I was out so late. I, too, have a brother, though I don't think he's ever done anything so awful as to speak to a horrible Armstrong."

Jessie thought that perhaps she should be insulted, but Marnie laughed and Jessie could not help smiling. "I don't think I'm horrible. And I don't think you're so horrible either—for a MacDuff."

Marnie laughed again. "Perhaps we could be friends. Perhaps no one would have to know. We could meet here next week and learn more about each other."

Jessie was about to answer, but suddenly she heard a noise behind her. "Father has probably sent men out to find me. I must go. But I will meet you here a week from tonight."

"Yes," said Marnie. "In one week."

The two parted, but a week later they met again. Leaving their horses to graze in the woods, they walked amid the trees and talked.

"Whatever started this foolish feud between our

families in the first place?" Jessie asked.

Marnie shrugged. "I don't think anyone even remembers for certain."

"Then it is time to end it," Jessie said.

"I wish we could. Oh look," said Marnie, "black currants. If my mother were here she would boil the currant leaves and make an ointment that's good for cuts and wounds. She's a great healer, you know."

Jessie scowled. "My mother died five years ago, right after Douglas was born. But..." she said, and smiled, "if my aunt Agnes were here she would pick the currants and bake some tarts."

"And my father would eat them," Marnie said with a laugh. "There's nothing he likes better than sweets, and my mother never bakes tarts." She stopped and turned toward her new friend. "It seems there is much our families could learn from each other."

"Yes," said Jessie. "So let's learn."

From then on, the girls secretly met every week. And each week their friendship grew. Meanwhile, the feud between their families continued, stronger than ever.

One night a band of MacDuff men crept onto Armstrong land and stole some sheep.

A few nights later the Armstrongs stole ten head of fat cattle from the MacDuffs.

The MacDuffs, in turn, raided the Armstrong's herds. That night Jessie's little brother, Douglas, was out exploring the hills in the moonlight. He was not with his big sister this time, since he wanted to prove to Jessie that he was a brave warrior. So when he saw the raiders, he crept through the ferns until he was very near one man. Then he drew his wooden sword and jumped up. The man he attacked was surprised by the small figure that seemed to appear out of nowhere. He swung wildly with his sword and nicked the boy's arm.

Douglas gasped in pain. His arm burned like fire. He stumbled backward. The man with the sword followed slowly. "I'm sorry. I didn't realize you were just a lad," he said, but Douglas was terrified now. Spinning around, he raced toward home and his father.

"They will pay!" yelled Lord Armstrong.

Jessie awoke because of the noise and hurried down the wooden stairs. Douglas was huddled up near the fire in the great hall where they ate. But above the blanket that was wrapped about him, she could see that his arm was bandaged.

"What happened?" she whispered.

"It was the MacDuffs!" her father raged. "They have raided our herds again. But this time they have wounded my son too. And now they will pay!"

"What will you do?" she asked.

"I will hurt someone that is as dear to Lord MacDuff as my son is to me," he said.

"But..." Jessie managed to take a step closer. She loved her father, and she knew he loved her, but when he was angry, it frightened her. "Perhaps they did not mean to hurt Douglas. Perhaps it was a mistake."

"Yes, it certainly was a mistake," Jessie's father thundered. "A mistake MacDuff will sorely regret when his own son is wounded."

Jessie gasped. Her father meant to hurt Marnie's brother. Then the MacDuffs would wound an Armstrong. And then, perhaps, the Armstrongs would kill a MacDuff.

"No, Father, please," she pleaded. "Don't do this. There must be another way to settle this."

Her father stared at her and in his eyes she saw his sadness. "This is the way it must be," he said. "I will have an eye for an eye and a tooth for a tooth. Everything they do to us, we will do to them."

Jessie held her breath. "Everything?" she asked.

"Yes," vowed her father. "Everything they do to the Armstrongs we will do to the MacDuffs, and more."

That afternoon Jessie was supposed to meet Marnie, but her father ordered her to stay in the castle. Jessie wanted to obey him, but she knew the only way to prevent more trouble was to speak to her friend. So she sneaked out when no one was looking.

A few minutes later, she was racing Flint bareback through the woods. Branches grabbed at her. They scratched her hands until the wounds bled, but she knew what she had to do.

"Marnie!" Jessie gasped. She pulled Flint to a halt. "I'm so glad you came."

Marnie looked pale and worried. "I listened while the men were talking. I know a boy was hurt and I am sorry."

"Douglas's arm is badly cut." Jessie wiped the blood from the back of her hand onto the skirt of her gown. She had no time to worry about herself now.

"It was your brother who was wounded?" Marnie asked.

"Yes. He crept from his room to go exploring in the hills. It's all my fault—I was the one who taught him how to sneak from the castle without anyone knowing. And now he's hurt because of it."

Marnie shook her head. "It's not your fault, Jessie. Oh! I hate this ridiculous feud. If our families were friends, my mother could heal Douglas' arm."

"That's just what I came to talk to you about," Jessie

said. "If we don't do something to stop this feud, some-one else will be hurt. Maybe it will be a MacDuff. Maybe it will even be your brother. My father has vowed to get revenge."

"But what can we do?" asked Marnie. "We're not the lords of our clans."

"No, we're not lords," Jessie said. "But we're smart enough to know this feud must end. And I know how we can end it."

Jessie didn't sleep well that night. Nightmares haunted her. But when she walked to the drawbridge the next morning, she made herself act as if nothing were different.

"Good morning, Malcom," she said to the watch-man. "Will you let me out so I can—" She stopped talk-ing as she gazed out at the bridge. A large jar stood there. She knew, then, that Marnie had convinced her mother to help with their plan. But she pretended to know noth-ing. "What is that sitting on the bridge?"

"Why, it looks like a jug of some sort," Malcom said in surprise.

"Let's see what it is," suggested Jessie.

In a minute Malcom held the jar in his hands. Lifting the cloth that covered it, he peered inside. "I don't know what it is," he said, "but it smells of herbs."

"There's a note," said Jessie, lifting up the piece of leather with writing on it.

"What does it say?"

Jessie was proud of the fact that she could read. Many people in her clan couldn't. "It says, 'This is an ointment to heal the lad's arm. Put it on the wound twice a day.' And it is signed, 'MacDuff.'"

Malcom raised his brows in surprise. "You'd best take that to our lord right away," he said.

When Jessie found her father, he scowled down at the note she handed him. He read it aloud, then read it again. "What kind of trick is this?" he asked.

"Maybe it's not a trick," Jessie said. "Maybe the MacDuffs just want to help."

"The MacDuffs never want to help," he said. "This stuff will probably only make Douglas' arm worse. The herbs in it could be poison. I'm throwing it out."

"No," Jessie pleaded. "Please. Look, I have a scratch on my hand. Let me put some of the ointment on that. If it doesn't get worse, we can try it on Douglas' wound."

Jessie's father reluctantly agreed. She smeared the fragrant stuff onto her hand. By evening her scratch looked better.

That night they covered Douglas' wound in the ointment and wrapped it in a bandage. By morning his arm didn't hurt as much and the swelling had gone down.

Jessie looked up from Douglas' arm and into her father's eyes. "Well," she said, trying to be brave, "I guess it's time you fulfilled your vow."

"What vow?" Lord Armstrong demanded.

"You said that whatever the MacDuffs do, you will do back plus more."

"What are you talking about, lass? I meant that I would make them pay for their crimes."

"You vowed that you would do the same thing they did," she reminded him.

"But..." Her father paced across the great hall. "That's nonsense. We don't even know how to make this healing ointment."

"Then give them something else," Jessie said. "Something nice."

Her father stared at her for a second. "Don't be foolish," he said.

"So your promises mean nothing?" Jessie asked.

"Of course I keep my promises," he said, looking angry.

"Then give them something good," Jessie pleaded.

That night, Lord Armstrong himself sneaked across MacDuff land. But this time he hadn't come to steal. Instead, he left a basket not far from the castle wall. In it was a bolt of fine velvet cloth and a note that read, "This is for the MacDuffs, from the Armstrongs."

Jessie was too nervous to sleep that night or the night after that. But when she hurried down to the gate a day later, she found a basket on the bridge. The basket was lined with the green cloth of the MacDuff clan and was filled with plump black currants. She took them to the kitchen where Aunt Agnes made them into sweet, crusty tarts.

That night Lord Armstrong took the tarts to the MacDuffs, but when he bent to set them on the bridge, the lord of the MacDuffs stepped out of hiding.

The two men stared at each other.

"I have heard that your son was wounded," said Lord MacDuff, "and I am sorry. But I am glad that we have been tricked into ending this feud."

"Tricked?" asked Lord Armstrong. "How do you mean?"

"I've discovered that our daughters have been meeting in the woods. It seems they have become friends."

"Jessie knows that is forbidden," Lord Armstrong said. "She would never sneak out to—" But then he stopped to listen. From the darkness, they could hear whispers. "Who's out there?" he called.

Jessie and Marnie stepped from their hiding place.

They had followed their fathers there.

Lord Armstrong's mouth fell open. "Jessie!" he said in surprise. "My daughter would sneak out, it seems."

"Yes, Father," she said quietly. "I would do almost anything to end the feud between the Armstrongs and the MacDuffs."

For a moment her father didn't speak, but then he nodded. Walking forward, he offered Lord MacDuff his hand in friendship. "It seems our daughters are wiser than we. For them we must end this feud."

"Yes, we will end it for them," said Lord MacDuff. Then he sniffed. Lord Armstrong was still holding the basket of the sweet currant tarts and the delicious smell was strong in the night air. "We will become friends for the sake of our children and for a taste of the sweet-smelling pastry in your basket. Come, we will eat the sweets together while our daughters decide what other ideas they have for the future."

"As a matter of fact," Jessie said as she winked at Marnie, "we've thought of several things already."

The Royal Joust

AN ORIGINAL STORY BY BRUCE LANSKY

Lady Rowena looked at the empty chair at the breakfast table and then at Lindsey. "Where is your brother? If he doesn't hurry up, he'll be late for the tournament."

"Don't worry, Mother. Reggie won't miss the finals of the Royal Joust. I'll see to that," Lindsey answered.

When she knocked on Reggie's bedroom door, Lindsey thought she heard a moan. As she opened the door, she noticed that Reggie's curtains were drawn. He was still in bed. Stepping into the room, she realized he was moaning—and talking to himself.

"Oh, no! I can't move!" Reggie repeated this lament over and over.

"You can't stay in bed, Reggie. Today is the last day of the tournament, so you'd better roll your aching body out of bed and into your armor. Then ride over to North Hampton by noon, or you'll be disqualified."

"I want to, but I can't. I was sideswiped by Sir Garth's horse yesterday. I have no idea how I stayed in my saddle. Now I can't ride, I can't walk, I can't even get out of bed," explained Reggie.

"Reggie, today is the last day of the tournament, and you're still undefeated. This is your big chance. At least give it a try."

"Sorry," said Reggie, "I hate to let you down. Would you mind riding to North Hampton to tell the tournament officials I'm withdrawing from the competition?"

"No problem, Reggie. I was planning to go anyway, to watch you win. No one in the tournament has worked harder than you. I wish I could take your place and bring back a trophy for you."

"So do I!" said Reggie. "Too bad they don't let girls compete."

Lindsey thought about what he said. It bothered her that Reggie would have to drop out of the tournament on the final day. She and Reggie had been training all year. Every day, weather permitting, Reggie's page, Giles, would help them suit up in armor and hoist them onto chargers so they could joust with padded lances. Reggie was bigger and stronger than Lindsey, but Lindsey was a skilled rider, better able to guide her horse to precisely the right place at the right time. She was almost impossible to hit, let alone unseat. And Giles knew enough to keep his mouth shut about a girl learning the knightly arts.

"You don't mind if I borrow your charger for the trip, do you?" asked Lindsey.

"No problem," Reggie responded, even though it was unusual to ride a charger to town. "Lightning could use the exercise."

"Thanks, Reggie. I'll send them a message they won't soon forget."

Lindsey explained to her mother that Reggie had asked her to let the tournament officials know he was unable to compete. Then she hurried to find Giles, for without a page to help her, she couldn't put her plan into action. Giles helped Lindsey put on Reggie's suit of armor and saddle up Lightning. Together, they set off at a trot on the road to North Hampton.

Lindsey and Giles reached North Hampton just as the tournament was about to begin. The crowd milled about in a festive mood while the knights were hoisted onto their horses. No one noticed that Lindsey (disguised as Reggie) was already mounted.

Anticipation built as each contestant rode onto the field. There would be three rounds of competition with eight contestants in the first round, four in the second, and two in the third. Lindsey had drawn Sir Wilton, one of the tallest knights on the circuit, as her first opponent.

With her helmet on and her visor down, Lindsey rode past the tournament officials, dipping her lance in the traditional salute to the king and queen. Then she lined up in Reggie's place at the edge of the field, opposite Sir Wilton. Trumpets blew a fanfare, and the tournament was under way.

On the first pass, Lindsey ducked under Sir Wilton's lance and managed to strike him on the shoulder. Although Sir Wilton was stunned, he remained in his saddle.

On the second pass, Lindsey guided Lightning inside toward Sir Wilton, whose horse shied away. Sir Wilton dropped his lance as he grabbed for the reins with both hands to gain control of his horse. That's when Lindsey's lance struck him and knocked him out of his saddle.

As was the custom, Lindsey rode up to where the king and queen were seated on the reviewing stand and again lowered her lance. A murmur of surprise went through the crowd when she did not lift her visor. Lindsey didn't care; she'd made it to the second round.

Her next opponent was Sir Rockwell, last year's champion. As Lindsey lined up at the end of the field opposite him, she wondered how she could possibly unseat such a seasoned opponent. The trumpets blared, and both horses galloped toward each other at breakneck pace.

Suddenly, Lindsey reigned in Lightning. The horse whinnied and dug in its heavy hooves. Sir Rockwell swung his lance away to avoid hitting Lightning, because injuring a horse meant instant disqualification. But Lindsey kept her lance trained on Sir Rockwell as he swept past her. The blow hit him squarely. He fell hard and didn't get up. Sir Rockwell seemed unconscious as his page carried him off the field, but a bucket of cold water quickly revived him.

Again Lindsey saluted the king and queen. Again she kept her visor shut. This time the crowd buzzed. People wondered why "Reggie" would not acknowledge the praise of the royal couple and the applause of the crowd by showing his face.

As Lindsey watched the other semifinalists compete, she saw Sir Gavilan unhorse his opponent in a single pass. The crowd cheered as Sir Gavilan lifted up his visor and lowered his lance to the king and queen. Clearly, he would be the crowd's favorite in the finals.

As both Lindsey and Sir Gavilan mounted their horses for the final round, he called to her, "If you won't open your visor, I'll just have to knock your helmet off."

Lindsey rode to her end of the field without saying a word. "Tongue-tied?" Sir Gavilan called out. Again, Lindsey didn't answer.

As the trumpets blared to start the final round, Sir Gavilan took off at a full gallop. But Lindsey merely trotted toward him, then stopped. Sir Gavilan was puzzled and lowered his lance. Lindsey suddenly spurred Lightning forward and would have scored a direct hit on Sir Gavilan had he not blocked her lance with his shield. He slipped to the right and almost lost his balance, but he managed to hang onto his horse with his strong legs.

Sir Gavilan's smile had been knocked off his face. He was worried as he prepared for the second pass. At the sound of the trumpets, the horses surged toward each other once again. This time, Sir Gavilan did not drop his guard. He kept his lance aimed directly at Lindsey. And even though Lindsey swerved toward him, he did not lower his lance.

Instead of trying to strike him with her own lance, Lindsey put all her strength and that of Lightning behind her shield as it met Sir Gavilan's lance. Shield crashed against lance with terrible force, and the blow knocked the lance out of Sir Gavilan's hand. It clattered, useless, to the ground.

Without a lance, Sir Gavilan had to draw his sword for the third pass; he was now at a distinct disadvantage. Bravely he drove his horse toward Lindsey, trying to get close enough to strike. But Lindsey swerved away to maintain her advantage and struck Sir Gavilan with her lance, bouncing him out of the saddle.

She had won. The tournament was over.

To a rising swell of cheers, Lindsey rode to the reviewing stand and waved to acknowledge the ovation. Without lifting her visor, she dismounted and bowed to the king and queen. The queen then presented the winner's trophy to Lindsey, who held it above her head as the crowd applauded thunderously. Then Lindsey mounted Lightning and rode around the field, holding the trophy aloft. When she returned to the reviewing stand, Lindsey handed the trophy back to the head judge so it could be engraved and happily galloped toward home.

That evening, a tournament official arrived at Lindsey's home and asked to see Sir Reginald. Lady Rowena greeted him instead, introducing herself and adding, "Reggie is in no condition to see any visitors. Please state your business to me."

"I am Sir William, head judge of the Royal Joust. I am here to present the championship trophy to Sir Reginald. His name has been engraved in silver upon it."

"I'm afraid you're mistaken, sir. Reggie had to drop out. He has been in bed all day."

Sir William was taken aback. "This is quite confusing.

We all watched Sir Reginald win three jousts, unseating Sir Wilton, Sir Rockwell, and Sir Gavilan. The queen herself presented the trophy."

"Are you sure it was Reggie?" asked Lady Rowena.

"Well, he was riding the same horse he's been on all week, and wearing his usual armor — "

"But did you ever see his face?" interrupted Lady Rowena.

"Now that you mention it, Sir Reginald caused quite a stir by refusing to lift his visor before the king and queen. Rather odd, if you ask me," Sir William replied.

"Lindsey! Come here this minute!" Lady Rowena's voice rang throughout the castle. Lindsey appeared so quickly, she must have been nearby listening to the conversation.

"Lindsey, didn't you inform Sir William that Reggie was injured and would have to drop out of the tournament?"

"No, Mother, I did not."

"Did you ride to North Hampton on Reggie's horse, Lightning?"

"Yes, Mother, I did."

"You weren't, by any chance, wearing Reggie's armor, were you?"

Lindsey looked first at her mother, then at Sir William. "Yes, Mother, I was."

Lady Rowena smiled at her daughter. "Lindsey, I'm

proud of you." Turning to Sir William, she said, "It is my pleasure to inform you that my daughter, Lindsey, and her brother, Reginald, have won the Royal Joust together."

"This is quite irregular! In fact, it's…it's…unheard of!" Sir William stammered.

Now it was Lindsey's turn to speak. "You would not have allowed me to compete if I had asked to take Reggie's place. So I took his place and kept my visor down so I would not be recognized."

Sir William frowned.

"Sir William, I would remind you of your duty as head judge to congratulate the winners," said Lady Rowena with a broad smile.

Sir William shook Lindsey's hand grudgingly. "By all means, congratulations are in order," he replied.

"I don't suppose you'd mind taking the trophy back and engraving Lindsey's name next to Reggie's?" Lady Rowena asked.

"Under the circumstances, I don't believe I have a choice," sputtered the befuddled judge.

Lindsey was dying to tell Reggie that they had won the Royal Joust together, but he could not be roused from a very deep sleep. So the good news would have to wait till morning.